Museum Nocturnus:

Monster Tales From Valley Falls

By

Jason Brannon

Copyright © 2022 Jason Brannon

This book is a work of fiction. Names, characters, places and incidents are either the product of the author's imagination or are used fictitiously. Any resemblance to actual events or locales or persons, living or dead, is entirely coincidental.

ISBN: **9798352827826**

All rights reserved, including the right of reproduction in whole or in part in any form.

This book is for Elijah Nicholas-a great son and skilled monster hunter. Let's see how you do with the monsters in this book!

I love you, buddy!

Contents

The Thief	1
Antibodies	16
The Thief, An Interlude	35
Old Ezra	37
Intermission	60
Running Toward Eden	63
Mother Mary	82
Intermission II	97
The Trophy	100
Quartet	112
Part I: Trapped	*112*
Part II: Escape	*114*
Part III: The Sea's Revenge	*119*
Part IV: Aftershock	*127*
Part V: The Truth	*136*
Part VI: The End	*141*
The Museum Strikes Back	148
About the Author	154

The Thief

To the casual observer who might drive down Cypress Lane and glance over at the sprawling three-story, multi-gabled Victorian-style mansion with the peeling white paint and slightly sagging wrap-around porch, it would seem like just another old house in need of major renovations. Mostly, that's true. But it's much more than a house. Or at least it is now. Only the wooden sign on the front lawn displaying the words "Museum Nocturnus" in a spiky black Gothic font provides any hint that the building's true purpose is something much stranger than to provide a simple residence for a sizable Valley Falls family.

It started out as an orphanage in the early years of Valley Falls. With fifteen bedrooms, an enormous dining hall, a cavernous kitchen, parlor, laundry, and six full bathrooms, the structure was built to give those unfortunate children with no parents a place to live until suitable arrangements with relatives or a foster family could be made. Eventually, a state-run orphanage was built, and all of the children were transferred there, leaving the mansion vacant and without a purpose.

A wealthy businessman from town named Silas Farnsworth bought the orphanage and tried his hand at turning it into a bed and breakfast. Silas's endeavor was successful for a while, but eventually, business went south, prompting him to sell. It was a story that would become prevalent and familiar over the years. Nothing in Valley Falls ever stayed shiny and new for long.

From there, the mansion changed hands numerous times. For a time, it was a private schoolhouse, a makeshift hospital after the original St. George's burned completely to the ground, a church, a gambling hall, a farmhouse restaurant, and even a brothel. If the walls of the house on Cypress Lane could talk, they would tell a patchwork story that spanned decades and spoke of sadness and loss, love and lust, happiness, faith, jealousy, triumph, rage, and every other emotion found somewhere on the spectrum of the human condition.

Babies had been born in the mansion. People had died there. Fortunes had been made and lost inside the mansion's walls. Love had blossomed in some cases. In others, the flames of lust were stoked behind closed doors. Faith had been discovered, lost, and found again. Each room in the house could tell a thousand different stories, and the ghosts of days gone by haunted the place.

Today, the house on Cypress Lane wasn't really a house. It had been transformed into a museum dedicated to the macabre, the creepy, the bizarre, and the supernatural. It housed artifacts that no other museum cared about or would be willing to display. Museum Nocturnus not only dealt in high strangeness but put it on full display for the world to see and admire. Exhibits had been carefully curated to tell the stories of serial killers, witches, madmen, cult members, and those who thrived in the darkness. It was a display dedicated to the weird, and the spotlights here were all firmly pointed at the darkness.

Max Garfield tiptoed carefully through a particular section of the museum called the Hall of Murderers. As he crept past portraits of some of the city's most well-known killers, he couldn't help thinking that taking this job might have been a bad idea. It seemed like a ridiculous notion to steal any of the items on display here, but it was obviously important to the one who had hired him. The amount of money he had been offered to undertake this heist was enough to make him overlook the eccentricities of the job. Everything had seemed so straightforward when considered in the light of day. But it was well past midnight now, and Max couldn't shake the feeling that he was being watched even though he knew good and well that he was the only one here. He had made certain of it. Despite the lack of any real evidence to suggest Max was in trouble, the idea of breaking into Museum Nocturnus and stealing some sort of old, moldy exhibit piece no longer seemed like a slam dunk.

The museum's security was a piece of cake to disable, but Max felt nervous, unsure of himself. Signs were posted everywhere that said, "Beware! Our items are protected." It seemed like an odd declaration. Of course, there were cameras and alarms in the museum, but somehow, Max didn't think that was what the statement meant. *Protected* was a strange word to use that suggested there were active methods in place to prevent the theft of the exhibits. Security cameras and alarms weren't capable of protecting anything. They were simply ways of monitoring the comings and goings inside the museum. No! The word *protected* indicated that the museum had a defense of some sort.

"You're overthinking this, Max," he told himself. "Just get a move on. The sooner you start this, the sooner you finish."

He crept deeper into the Hall of Murderers. The hair on his arms and the back of his neck stood at attention. This place felt wrong.

The paintings of deviant killers lined both sides of the hall, glaring at him, seeming to follow his movements with their lifeless eyes. Max couldn't dismiss the idea that one of the maniacs might step out of their portrait at any moment and sharpen their knives on his soft flesh. He stared up at the painting of a madman named Gemini and was certain that the fiend in the black-hooded robe and greasepaint was watching him, waiting for just the right moment to creep out of the shadows to do some bloody work with his hammer. Gemini's face had been drawn with a faint, amused smile. Max couldn't help thinking that the killer, who had once based the patterns of his killing cycles on the astrological star chart, was amused by his fear.

Max quickly turned away, unwilling to look at the ghastly art any longer than he absolutely had to. The art wasn't the goal of the heist anyway. As he turned, he caught a glimpse of himself in one of the glass display cases, and the sight surprised him. His normal icy, blue-eyed gaze had thawed a bit, becoming lukewarm with insecurity. His hair, which was usually well-coiffed and glued to his scalp with a gel that smelled like tea tree oil, stuck up in unruly black patches on his head. His face was a mask of doubt and paranoia, and his gaze darted back and forth between the portraits of so many serial killers. Sweat trickled down his brow, and yet he shivered. He had been a cat burglar for many years, and he couldn't ever remember feeling like this. Not even during those first few jobs at the beginning of his career. Still, he was a professional and would finish what he had started. He pressed on, just wanting to get this over with.

Despite feeling jittery and nervous, Max still noticed something in the Hall of Murderers that was likely the direct result of so many years of training to pay close attention to detail. The same artist was responsible for all of the commissions in the hall. The painted scrawl in the lower right-hand corner of each painting read only, "*B. Thorn.*" Max made a mental note to learn more about B. Thorn at some point in the future. While the paintings were horrific, they were also masterful and would likely fetch a fine price with the right buyer. If this first heist was successful, he could always come back.

The Hall of Cursed Toys was the next stop on the journey to his ultimate destination, and the sight of so many bizarre items displayed in the half-light was almost enough to make him want to return to the discomfort of the Hall of Murderers. The toys all sat on lighted pedestals, but the world around them was black. After hours, all of the additional overhead lighting was turned off, making it seem as if each of the toys was floating in a sea of darkness. As Max navigated the hall, he half expected something scaly and amphibian to slither out of the shadows, wrap itself around his leg, bury a dozen barbed suckers into his tender flesh, and drag him away to some dismal fate.

"Take a breath, Max," he told himself. "This is just another gig. You got this."

Of course, no gig he'd ever worked before involved one of those creepy monkeys that stared at you with wide-eyed lunacy while banging its cymbals together in an unsettling cadence. The Hall of Cursed Toys was quiet at the moment, almost preternaturally so, and Max couldn't help thinking that he would likely go into cardiac arrest if the monkey on the lighted pedestal suddenly came to life and started clapping its paws. But the monkey wasn't the worst or only thing that set his nerves on edge. Far from it. As he glanced around the room, he also saw a robot with wide saucer-like eyes that was reported to speak in static-filled bursts of prophecy despite having no batteries, a doll named Sally that talked in cryptic riddles and was rumored to be inhabited by the spirit of a murdered girl, and a pair of special joke glasses that was supposed to allow you to catch glimpses of the other side.

Max didn't take the time to examine any of the other items in the Hall of Cursed Toys. Instead, he pressed onward, determined to reach his final destination.

The Hall of Haunted Items was next in this hellish, paranormal junkyard, and Max had to resist the urge to squeeze his eyes tightly shut and run at top speed to his ultimate goal. Above all else, however, he was a professional, and he forced himself to walk at a calm pace, even though that was the last thing he wanted to do. It felt like the devil himself was standing right behind him, breathing his sulfurous breath onto Max's collar. The thought put ice water in his veins.

This place was just downright creepy. That's all you could say about it.

One exhibit in this particular hall was dedicated to an old, dirty dot-matrix printer that could supposedly print hidden facts. In that way, it served as a sort of electronic oracle. Or at least that's what the description claimed. Under another dingy spotlight was an antiquated camera that had the ability to imprint events from the future onto its film. To the casual observer, most of the items here looked like your everyday, run-of-the-mill pile of crap that had been discarded from someone's basement. Max still wasn't sure that wasn't what all of this was. It was like he had unwittingly stumbled onto Satan's garage sale.

Surely, none of the claims were real. The stories were what made these items interesting. Not any sort of magic powers they might possess. He didn't believe in that stuff anyway.

Max moved between the exhibits, careful not to touch any of them just in case their bad juju might somehow rub off on him. Thankfully, he didn't have far to go. His destination was just ahead.

Because of the tremendous success they had seen thus far, the owners of Museum Nocturnus had decided to go a little further and open a new exhibit, this one more grandiose and more outlandish than the three before it. The Hall of Monsters was a shrine to tooth and claw, and this was where the job was. This was where the person calling themselves The Antiquarian had sent him.

Even now, he didn't know much about the person who had hired him. Everything had been done anonymously through message boards on the dark web. It was the only way to do business nowadays if you were a discerning criminal. After all, it wasn't like he could just post wanted ads in the classified section of the newspaper advertising his services as a cat burglar.

The buyer had initially contacted him via email and referred to himself as "The Antiquarian." It was a strange moniker. The word referred to one who collected old things or amassed antiques. Of course, some of the things in the museum would technically fall into this category, but these weren't the sorts of items most people made a habit of collecting. Who on earth would want a pen that could channel the spirits of long-dead writers? This place was too strange for Max's tastes, but The Antiquarian had done his best Godfather impression and made him an offer he couldn't refuse. The money was too good to pass up. And so here he was, trembling for no good reason and wanting nothing more than to run back to the safety of his apartment where he would immediately secure all of the locks and bury himself under a mound of blankets in his warm, cozy bed, cradling his pistol against his chest. He felt like a young boy again, scared of his own shadow and longing for the safety of his mother's bosom. Maybe it was best to get what he came for and get out of Museum Nocturnus.

Of course, to do so meant exploring the newly launched Hall of Monsters. Accessing the Hall of Monsters, in this case, meant walking through a giant demonic mouth filled with jagged, bloodstained fangs that served as the doorway. Max cautiously touched one of the teeth and was surprised to find that it was quite sharp. What surprised him even more was the sticky red lacquer that strangely mimicked the feel of dried blood. There was no way that that's what it was. Still…

He cautiously stepped into the open mouth of the scarlet-faced demon. He half expected Virgil to step out of the shadows and offer to take him on a journey down into Dante's Nine Circles of Hell. Yet, nothing happened. It felt like the entire hall was holding its breath, waiting for just the right moment to exhale and spring the trap on him that was most assuredly waiting for him here.

As its name implied, the Hall of Monsters was a monument dedicated to every sort of nightmarish creature that the discerning paranormal enthusiast could conjure up in their darkest nightmares. The exhibits were a mixture of Bigfoot print casts, grainy photos of blurry shapes that may or not have been proof of the existence of the

Mothman, one of the traveling wagons from noted monster exhibitionist Captain Jack Omaha's Cryptozoological Fair and Freak Show, and even the body of what was purported to be an alien from Area 51 (although why the government still hadn't confiscated it was anybody's guess). However, the crown jewel of the exhibit was something much bigger, much grander.

Max studied the exhibit with some curiosity and wondered why The Antiquarian was so interested in all of this. Why was this worth fifty grand? On the surface, everything in the exhibit looked like something you might pick up for a few bucks at a rummage sale. But, like everything else here in Museum Nocturnus, there had to be more to it.

The centerpiece of the Hall of Monsters was an exhibit dedicated to Marcus Magnusson. According to the placard in front of the exhibit, Magnusson was the preeminent monster hunter in Valley Falls. Max thought the notion humorous, as if monster hunters were so prevalent in Valley Falls that there was a ranking system for them. Of course, Valley Falls was a weird place. Maybe he just hadn't turned over enough rocks to find all of the dark secrets that lingered there.

The man in the exhibit photo that had to be Magnusson was a burly, gruff-looking man with a dimpled chin, a heavily waxed mustache, and a scar that cut across one cheek. One eye was a bright, piercing blue, and the other was a deep green glass eye. With long dirty blonde hair that fell to his shoulders and a lumberjack's sturdy build, Magnusson looked like a Viking. What ruined the illusion was the pith helmet, the beige safari shirt, cargo pants, big brown belt, and boots that he wore. It was like Thor had suited up to take a trip into the heart of the Amazon. One part Norse god, one part jungle explorer, Magnusson definitely cut quite the figure.

The exhibit itself consisted of shadow boxes filled with what were presented to be the unbelievably large fangs from an enormous snake, the chitinous scales of a race of fish people, the claws of a bloodthirsty demon, the hair of a chupacabra, and dozens of other bits of highly strange ephemera collected from decades of monster hunting that might only be appreciated in a place like Museum Nocturnus. Magnusson's weapons were on display as well. Although there were a few firearms in the mix, it was clear that he preferred blades of all shapes and sizes over guns. Swords, sabers, daggers, scythes, and axes were displayed prominently with the spotlights positioned to highlight the runes and ancient carvings prevalent on each one that supposedly gave them some sort of supernatural advantage over the monsters they were used to fight. Then there was the glass eye on a pedestal in the center of the room.

This was what he had been instructed to steal.

According to the description on the plaque mounted beneath the display, anyone who used the eye could glimpse the hidden details of any item they possessed. The most widely accepted account of the eye's origin was that it had been a scrying crystal belonging to one of the original

Valley Falls witches whose specific talent involved summoning the dark creatures of the woods and using them to do her bidding. In an effort to conceal her deeds and preserve her dark secret, she reduced the size of the crystal through much physical manipulation and turned it into an eye that could be used for divination. The stories about how Magnusson had acquired the eye were varied, but one detail was consistent. Magnusson was so convinced of the eye's abilities that he had gouged out one of his own eyes to make room for it. Then, gifted with the "second sight" it afforded him, he would use it to find out the details about whatever creature he was tracking. At that point, armed with accurate first-hand knowledge of the creature in question, including where it could be found and what its potential weaknesses were, he would have enough of an advantage to actively hunt it.

The placard explained:

"Over the years, numerous people have held Marcus's glass eye in one hand and been able to catch a first-hand glimpse of the mysterious creatures he hunted. Sometimes, these viewing experiences are harmless. Other times, the viewing experience is a bit more violent, showing tragedy and bloodshed. *What will you experience?*"

"What will I experience?" Max muttered. "This can't be real. But even if it is real, what in the world would The Antiquarian want with something like this?"

He studied the eye carefully. Under the glow of the spotlights, the eye looked very exotic and very expensive, like an onion skin swirl marble. A strange series of markings and etchings adorned the back of the eye, no doubt put there by the witch who made it. It looked like writing in a foreign language of some sort, but Max wasn't an expert in these types of things. All he could guess was that the etchings were potentially a spell or incantation of some sort that gave the glass eye its mystical properties.

He went back to his initial question of why The Antiquarian might want such a thing. He considered the implications of owning such an item if it did what the museum claimed it could do. An eye that could glimpse monsters that had been created by a witch? It sounded ridiculous... and amazing. If such a thing were possible, there was no question it would be worth the fifty grand The Antiquarian had offered him. He thought about how much money he could make if he happened to discover Bigfoot and be able to provide proof. Fifty grand was a drop in the bucket compared to what he could earn.

This raised the question of if the eye was genuine and Magnusson had used it, why hadn't he come forward with discoveries of any mythical bloodthirsty monsters? Either the eye was a hoax (which was the most likely answer), or Magnusson was a fraud (which was also very possible)... or both! Of course, there was only one way to find out. If the eye was nothing more than a pawn shop bauble, then he would hand-deliver it to The Antiquarian and collect a sizable paycheck for the night's work. If it was real, well, then that changed everything, didn't it?

Having already disabled the security system before entering the museum, Max had no trouble lifting the glass from the display and picking up the eye. It felt heavy in his hand, like a paperweight, far heavier than an eye should feel. It also felt galvanizing, as if a tiny electrical current ran through it.

What will you experience?

Max thought about his life for a moment. He lived alone, had virtually no friends, and lived out a meager existence in a tiny apartment. He didn't really experience anything. Not really. The only thrills he got came from stealing things, and those jobs were taken only out of necessity whenever funds got low. Maybe it was time he tested the waters of experience and discovered whether or not he could swim in those tumultuous currents.

"*Beware! Our items are protected*," the notices screamed at him in a bold, 100-point font.

Interpreting the signs' declaration as more of a challenge than a warning, Max made up his mind. "Screw it," he said, doing his best to will away the nervousness that was coiled in his gut like a serpent waiting to strike. "Let's see what all the fuss is about."

Not really knowing how this whole thing was supposed to work, he decided to try something and smashed the glass on one of the shadow boxes that contained artifacts collected throughout Magnusson's career. He glanced over the items that were mounted to a cream-colored cushion inside the box and chose one at random. It was a chunk of tree bark that was covered in a dark, oily goo. "Recovered from Easthaven Forest. Residue from creatures of unknown origin. Dangerous."

Museum Nocturnus

It seemed as good a place to start as any. Stepping out of the light into one of the unlit corners of the Hall of Monsters, Max sat down on the floor with his back against one wall. He clutched the tree bark in one hand and the glass eye in the other. Then, he squeezed his eyes shut and tried to relax.

Immediately, the scene he witnessed in his mind's eye was filled with Technicolor images that sprang to life in a kaleidoscope of colors and shapes. It was the scene of an immense forest filled with towering Douglas fir trees that looked tall enough to scrape the clouds. Max even thought he could smell the scent of pine and felt a faint, crisp breeze on his cheeks. Opening his eyes, he looked around in amazement, searching for anything in the Hall of Monsters that could explain the smell or the sudden chill in the room. There was nothing. But the image of the forest was gone. He shut his eyes again, and it returned. This time, he heard birds chirping and men talking nearby. The sounds grew louder.

"What will you experience?" had been the question, and the word choice was apt. No longer was Max strictly inside the museum. Part of him was in the forest, and it was exhilarating.

With rapt attention, he watched the scene in his mind.

Little did he know, he was about to find out what was responsible for the dark goo on that chunk of tree bark.

This was the first of the things he experienced...

Antibodies

"You're not having second thoughts on me, are you, Doc? There's still a bear in Easthaven Forest that has your name written all over his hide."

Dr. Everett Grayton took off his camouflage cap for a moment and wiped his moonlit brow with the back of his sleeve. "You'll get your money, Jeff. Don't worry about that. I'm not backing out on you. I plan to see this through till the very end."

Jeff shifted his tobacco from one side of his mouth to another, apparently satisfied with the answer. "I shot Black Bart two or three times on past hunts, but that wasn't near enough to bring him down. We'll finish the job this time. I guarantee it."

Everett wasn't really paying attention anymore. He was listening to the heartbeat of the wilderness, the thrum of unseen life. If he'd had his stethoscope with him out here in the midst of nature, he might have detected a pulse. Yet even without the equipment, he knew the place was alive. Call it primal instinct or the result of years and years of experience. Out here in the wild, he didn't feel much like a doctor. He felt more like an intruder.

He could almost feel the sets of eyes watching him from the shadows. That probably had something to do with the fact that hunting bears without a permit was illegal. Of course, he knew he was overreacting and just being paranoid. However, strange things had been known to go down in Easthaven Forest. People had died out here. Strangely and without explanation. There were rumors of all sorts of things living in the deepest, darkest parts of Easthaven Forest that weren't part of the natural order. Things like the cryptid known only as Red Fang. Things that were worse than Red Fang. Maybe the eyes he felt upon him were responsible for all those deaths reported in the newspapers and not simply the result of a guilty conscience. Or maybe he was just jittery at the thought of getting arrested.

"Are you sure the park rangers will leave us alone?" he asked Jeff. "You promised me that." Jeff didn't respond at first. He was too busy emptying the tobacco from his mouth and replacing it with sunflower seeds.

"Curt Bell is the ranger around these parts. He and his wife have a new baby at home. I gave him a little money for diapers and formula to look over us for a day or two. I would expect that the bank account's been dwindling down to nothing since the birth, so the extra money will no doubt come in handy. He'll leave us alone. Besides, he's a friend of mine. We duck hunt together. If push comes to shove, he'll turn a blind eye to it all."

"You guarantee that?" Everett asked, still a bit skittish.

Jeff worked on a sunflower seed and spit out the hull with a big smile. Then, he hitched his pants up over his considerable gut. "Sure do," he said with a southern drawl. "I guarantee it."

Despite Jeff's 'Good Ol' Boy' assurances, Everett kept waiting for a ranger to spotlight them and order them to drop their weapons. All he got instead was the angry growl of a chainsaw biting into the tough bark of a nearby tree. The doctor jumped and looked nervously over at his guide. Jeff didn't seem to be shaken by the noise. Instead, he simply spat out another sunflower seed hull.

"What is that?" Everett asked, gripping his rifle tightly.

"Lumberjacks," Jeff said. "Timber pirates who haven't been able to get the proper permits. I think Curt gets money from them too. Don't worry about them, though. We're going somewhere else. I did a little scouting up this way before you arrived. I found a bear's den not too far away. I think that's where we'll find Black Bart. We'll leave the loggers alone, and they'll leave us alone. None of us are supposed to be out here doing what we're doing. That breeds a certain sort of respect among the sorts of folks that come out here in the dead of night to escape the eyes of the law."

"Let me guess," Everett said, "you guarantee all that too?"

"You read my mind," Jeff said, cracking another seed with his teeth.

Museum Nocturnus

"So, let's get a move on," the doctor said, running a hand through his thinning gray hair. "I'm ready to get this over and done with."

"The hunt is always more fun than the kill," Jeff said with a smile that showed only a fraction of the number of teeth that should have been there. "Kind of like Christmas. The build-up beats the presents every time."

"I think this may be my last trip into the woods," Everett explained. "The thrill of the hunt isn't exactly a priority for me this time. It was probably a mistake to come out here, but I can't back out now, can I?"

"Second thoughts?" Jeff asked. "Are you that worried about getting caught?"

Everett scanned the dark woods. He still couldn't shake the feeling that they weren't welcome or alone. He kept waiting on the night to simply fold up on them like a great shadowy blanket, smothering them and burying them in darkness for eternity. "Do you ever think that the wilderness would be more perfect if we weren't here? Mother Nature seems to keep everything in perfect balance until we arrive on the scene. Then it's like watching cancer eat away at a healthy body."

"You're not going all Greenpeace on me, are you, Doc?"

"No, just contemplative. I've had a lot on my mind lately. Don't forget I'm a physician. Those sorts of thoughts come naturally to me."

"That's why we're out here, Doc. To get away from whatever is on your mind. Escape a little."

"Maybe," Everett admitted. "Or maybe whatever is on my mind is the reason I'm out here in the first place. It just feels like we're intruders here, ruining whatever we touch."

Jeff sighed and tossed his seed package into a patch of moonlit oleander. He didn't even realize what he had done until Everett looked at him sternly.

"Sorry," Jeff said, realizing his mistake. "I guess I'm just making your case for you."

"We're like viruses ravaging a pristine specimen. Marauders that destroy everything we come in contact with. The lumberjacks are cutting down the forest. We're out here to shoot anything that moves. Murray Chemical has probably dumped tons and tons of hazmat in the streams. You can walk through here during daylight and find all kinds of trash that campers or other hunters have left behind. Coke cans. Empty shells. Garbage bags. Bottles of lighter fluid. Spent matches. Discarded contraception. Sunflower seed packets..."

"Doc, I think you've been spending too much time in the lab. We're just as much a part of nature as the trees and the animals. Nature has always been about the hunt. And the kill. I didn't take you for one of those 'Save the Planet' types."

"Nature hasn't ever been about sport. Killing, yes, but killing to survive. We're killing because we can, because we enjoy it, because we are the most destructive form of life on this planet. Think of cancer again, only on a grand scale."

"Why are you dwelling on cancer, Doc? The ole prostate giving you trouble?"

Everett took off his hat and ran a hand through his thinning gray hair. "My twenty-six-year-old daughter has cancer. She's got a fifty-fifty chance to live. We found out a week ago. They're giving her chemo and treating her as aggressively as possible. Maybe she'll pull out of it. Maybe she won't. Either way, it's made me reevaluate my entire life and everything I've believed thus far. Since we arrived, I haven't stopped thinking about what I came out here to do. We came to kill, and we won't settle for anything less. We're like a cancer on the world, eating away at resources, draining the earth of its life, of its essence. Maybe Jenny's disease is the natural world's way of getting back at me for all the nasty things I've done."

"I think you're overstating this a little, Doc," Jeff said. "We're only after one bear. Nothing more. If you want, we'll come back and plant a tree on the spot where we took him down. Or we'll buy a couple of doves and release them into the wild. Whatever."

"I've hunted zebra, lions, antelope, rhinos, deer, you name it. Not once have I ever felt guilty about pulling the trigger. It took this change in perspective to really put my actions under the microscope."

"Do you want to hunt, or don't you?" Jeff asked impatiently. It was clear he was out of his league in this sort of debate. "If you want to talk philosophy and morality, then you've got the wrong guy. I came out here to help you kill Black Bart. That's what you hired me for."

Everett cleared his throat, almost embarrassed by his declarations. "Yes, of course. Maybe I'm overreacting. Let's do this and get it over with."

Jeff tensed and clutched his rifle tightly. A worried look quickly washed over his face like a splash of putrid water. "That might have been an option to begin with. It's not now."

"What are you talking about?" Everett said over the buzz of chainsaws.

"Don't move a muscle," Jeff said. "There's something behind you. I think it's a bear."

It was all Everett could do to control himself and refrain from looking. But he trusted the fear on Jeff's face. Jeff slowly lifted his rifle and sighted something just over Everett's shoulder. "I think it might be Black Bart," he said.

"I'm about to turn around slowly and have a look for myself."

"Just don't get in my line of sight. If he charges, I'll have to shoot."

Everett nodded. When he turned around, he was face to face with a haggard, starving bear. Its jaws were thick with white foam, and its eyes were like smoldering embers. He could have counted the animal's ribs if not for fear of losing a hand. It had obviously been a while since it had eaten. It growled at them with its frothy mouth and then roared. A red patch of dried blood marked one flank like a painful birthmark.

"That's where I shot him the first time," Jeff said, amazed. "It's only been a week since I hunted him. There's no way he could have lost so much weight since then. He looks sick. Diseased, maybe."

The bear tried to stand up on its hind legs and roar as it had done so many times before against intimidated hunters. But those legs were no longer strong enough to support the weight. The bear fell over like a drunkard.

Jeff sighted the bear through his scope and was about to pull the trigger.

"There's not much skill involved in killing a bear that's almost dead," Everett said. There was a note of pleading in his voice that he himself didn't understand. He had never had any qualms before about killing defenseless animals. Why now? Maybe it was because this animal had done nothing to deserve its fate. Or maybe it was because he was hoping the disease that was slowly eating away at his daughter would have the same mercy on her that he was going to show the bear. He clung to the idea of a compassionate cancer, even though he knew it was foolhardy.

"Leave it alone," Everett said firmly. "I'll still pay you. As far as I'm concerned, you've made good on your promise to deliver Black Bart."

The bear made a sound that spoke of pain, of misery, of a quivering fear in the face of eternity. By now, the foam around his muzzle was as thick as shaving cream. Everett felt sorry for him. "It's not common with bears, but I think he's rabid," he said. "Maybe we should kill him after all. Put him out of his misery. Stop an epidemic before it breaks out."

But the bear still pawed at life as it would its next meal. It was dying now. Only the misery was left to be measured in minutes and hours. It managed to get to its feet and lumbered drunkenly into the woods.

"Come on," Jeff said. "We've got to follow it."

Everett nodded. For once, killing an animal would be an act of preservation rather than one of destruction.

Black Bart had a good head start on them, but it wasn't hard to follow his trail. The bear left a messy line of frothy saliva and blood on the carpet of pine needles.

"I still don't understand how he's gone downhill so fast," Jeff said as they ran through the woods. "He has changed dramatically in such a short amount of time. It's like-"

He was cut short by the bear's screaming. It was like listening to a woman on an operating table without the benefit of anesthesia. Neither of the men had ever heard anything like it before and went cold at the sound.

They found the bear a few hundred yards deeper into the woods. There was very little left to indicate the bloody mess before them had ever been a bear. It was like he'd been fed into a meat grinder and spit out. A fine coating of something resembling motor oil covered the raw meat. It glistened in the moonlight and smelled like a hundred rotten eggs baking in the summer sun.

Jeff threw up at the sight. He had gutted animals dozens of times, but this was different. This was worse. Everett managed to keep his supper down. It helped that he had seen the worst of human atrocity during his stint in the emergency room. He covered his mouth and nose with the neck of his hunting shirt.

"That bear didn't just die. He was killed savagely." Jeff said, wiping his mouth with the back of his hand. "What could have done that? And what's that black stuff all over the carcass?"

Everett studied the remains as calmly as he could, taking shallow breaths through the cloth of his shirt. "Maybe the wilderness stopped the threat of outbreak on its own?" he suggested.

"There's a wolf or something out here that did this. Period."

"A wolf?" Everett said. "No way a wolf could do something like this to a bear. That bear was an apex predator. He's at the top of the food chain."

"Not the top," Jeff said. "There's something else out here that is higher."

"Maybe we should just go and find those lumberjacks," Everett said, clearly disagreeing with the wolf theory. "Warn them that something's out here."

They walked through the forest like robbers in a house full of glass. Every now and then, they heard something behind them or at their flank. But when they shone their flashlights in that direction, there was never anything there. It was like they were being stalked by noisy ghosts. Of course, ghosts weren't capable of the kind of brutality necessary for systematically dismembering a thousand-pound bear.

The chainsaws provided a constant roar in the background. They were as much a part of the night as the symphony of chirruping crickets and hooting owls. Both men felt reassured by the fact that there were lumberjacks out here in the woods with them. Granted, Everett and Jeff were both well-armed, seasoned hunters. But there was a comfort to be had in the fact that there were other germs wreaking havoc in the body politic.

It was clear, however, that something was terribly wrong when they reached the logging camp. Only bits and pieces of the lumberjacks were left, looking like victims of their own machinery. Stumps were covered in blood and ragged meat and the gooey slime that looked like Havoline 10W40. The chainsaws continued to idle, like mechanical mourners at a backwoods wake.

"Good God," Jeff said, immediately loading a shell into his rifle. He turned to look around them, searching for the things that had killed six full-grown men.

"Still think it's a wolf?" Everett said coolly. It seemed that he was more comfortable around the human remains than he had been with the remains of Black Bart.

"It's something else," Jeff said, gasping for air. "I'll agree with you on that. I've heard stories about the sorts of things that live out here in Easthaven Forest. I've never much believed any of it until now."

A thought occurred to Everett that might explain what killed Black Bart and the loggers, but he didn't want to say it aloud. Jeff already thought he was crazy with all that talk of cancer and germs. But what if the talk wasn't crazy?

A couple of spare cans of gas mixed with 2-cycle oil sat nearby. Jeff quickly filled the tank of an eighteen-inch Stihl and started it on the second pull. He revved it up and held it above his head like a maniac in a horror movie. "Let's see something come at me like it did these guys." It was clear that he was scared out of his wits and trying hard to cover it up.

Everett brushed off one of the stumps that wasn't covered in gore and sat down, watching Jeff. "We'll have to camp here tonight, you know? We can't risk going back through the woods and risk getting ripped apart."

"We'll build a fire," Jeff said. "That should scare everything away. If it doesn't, we're well-armed."

Everett had his doubts but kept them to himself. He hadn't stopped thinking about the cancer analogy. It just seemed to fit the situation. Even the killings fit into that analogy.

"We should cover up the bodies," Everett suggested. "We don't want everything smelling the blood and coming around for dinner. There are too many scavengers out here."

Jeff nodded and sat the idling chainsaw down beside his loaded rifle. The loggers had placed a lot of their supplies underneath tarps to keep them dry in case of rain. Jeff used the tarps to cover up the worst of the atrocities. "That should do it," he said a little unevenly. It was clear that he was trying to be a man but finding it hard under the circumstances.

As if to prove that he was still in control of the situation, Jeff picked the Stihl up again and slashed through the tender trunk of an oak sapling.

"What are you doing?" Everett asked, aghast.

Jeff saw the look on Everett's face and stopped the chainsaw. "What's wrong with you?" he asked, more than a little puzzled. "I'm just blowing off some steam. It's been a stressful night. Or do I need to remind you of that?"

"The notion of cancer is what's wrong with me," Everett said as if that explained everything. "We're the cancer here. We destroy everything even if there isn't a reason."

"Here we go again," Jeff sighed. For the moment, his irritation outweighed his fear. "I think there is a homicidal maniac loose out here like the kind that terrorized Camp Grand Echo years ago. That's what killed the lumberjacks. But you obviously have a different thought. So go ahead and spill it. Say what you've got to say. I'll listen even if I don't agree with you."

"Think of us as viruses. We're invaders here in Easthaven Forest, destroyers of life, cancers bent on ravaging living tissues. If you go with that assumption, there could be consequences to our being here just as there were consequences for the rabid bear and for the lumberjacks."

"Explain," Jeff said as he pulled a pouch of tobacco out of his camouflage vest. He dropped the empty package on the ground and smiled at Everett as if to spite the doctor and his stupid theory. For the moment, he wasn't as scared as he had been earlier and was determined to put on a brave face.

"There are things in a normal healthy body to ward off infection, to fight germs and viruses. They are called antibodies. If these woods could be compared to a perfect physical specimen and we could be compared to a bunch of destructive pathogens invading the host, then couldn't it be possible that the wilderness has its own defenses? What if this body has its own antibodies?"

"I understand why you would assume that the forest wouldn't necessarily be thrilled to have the lumberjacks around. But what about Black Bart? He was a part of the forest."

"He was until he went rabid. Then he was just another germ threatening the health of the body. Just like the lumberjacks. Just like us."

"This makes no sense," Jeff said. "The forest isn't some all-knowing creature."

"It's an analogy," Everett argued. "But everything here is interconnected. Think of the food chain. Think of the cycle of decomposition. Everything here relies on everything else. In that way, it's like a body. And yes, I realize there aren't antibodies as such floating around in the ether. But figuratively speaking, there might be something out here that protects the sanctity of the wilderness. Something that eliminates any potential threats."

"Listen," Jeff said, holding one hand up.

Everett stopped talking. He heard it immediately. The crunch of leaves underfoot. The crackle of branches snapping beneath the weight.

"Maybe one of the loggers made it out alive and went for help," Jeff said hopefully. "Maybe that's the search party. Or maybe it's the killer."

"I don't like this," Everett said, peering deep into the darkness beyond the logging camp. At first, he didn't see anything. Just pooling shadows and the faint outline of things that he knew were trees. Would it be better if Jeff was right and a chainsaw-wielding maniac emerged with a wicked smile and a taste for blood? Such things were possible. But this felt different, wrong somehow.

"Something's out there," Jeff said. "I saw it move. There!" He pointed to the left at a moving group of shadows that seemed to dance and coalesce into something vaguely humanoid.

Jeff raised the chainsaw he had used to cut down the tree. "It's a man. See, I told you! Look at the shape!"

The black figure moved through the darkness like quicksilver, fluidly and silently. It headed toward them.

"Stop, or I'll make you sorry," Jeff shouted, his voice slightly higher in pitch.

The black figure took another step, moving out of the darkness beneath the canopy and into the meager light of the logging camp.

It wasn't a maniac, nor was it a lumberjack. It was quickly joined by other similar shapes.

They weren't even men. They were something else. Something inhuman and linked inexplicably to this forest.

"Antibodies," Everett hissed.

That description was as good as any other. They were like men made entirely of shadow, black save for the spatters of blood that marked their smooth nightmare forms. Bear blood. Human blood.

Sexless and featureless, the antibodies ambled rather than walked. Two of them bumped into each other, melded for a second, and then split apart again. It was like watching liquid mercury. Everett thought of the viscous black substance found on the carcasses of the bear and on the remains of the lumberjacks. He wondered if it was what passed for blood from these creatures. Or if they left some of themselves behind like saliva on a hunk of half-eaten meat.

Jeff was still holding the chainsaw in his hand when the darkness entered the moonlit clearing. They saw the damage he had done to the tree with the saw and came toward him slowly, like they had all the time in the world. Bits of dark bear fur stuck to their clawed hands. Jeff threw down the Stihl and picked up his rifle, firing off several rounds in succession. The antibodies absorbed the bullets harmlessly and expelled them like waste. The spent rounds fell silently onto the carpet of pine needles.

"Do something, Everett!" he screamed as the antibodies came for him. But Everett knew better than to interfere. This host was much stronger than the viruses that had invaded it.

The antibodies fell upon Jeff with claws like chunks of sharp obsidian, ripping him apart. The rifle fired several more times as Jeff's finger twitched in agony, but the bullets might as well have been rocks thrown by a third grader for all the good they did. Soon there wasn't a trace of the man left, save for a heap of raw, bloody meat, a few fillings, a belt buckle, a wad of keys, and a hunting knife that he'd had strapped to his thigh. It was almost as if he had been gobbled up by the night and spat back out. Nothing Everett had ever observed under a microscope could have prepared him for this.

Hoping to stay alive, he did the only thing he could and ran for his life. Briars ripped at his face. Branches tugged insistently at his clothes. Once he almost tripped over a fallen tree, but he didn't slow down. Jeff's truck wasn't too far. If he could just make it that far, he might have a chance.

His lungs were filled with fire, and his calves burned. But he didn't stop. Not for a second. His side cramped, and he felt like he might throw up. Yet, he knew that any sort of delay would bring about his downfall.

Hope filled him when the truck came into sight. He had just thought to himself that he might make it out of this after all when something grabbed his ankle and took him to the ground. Everett screamed as he fell, certain that he was a goner. Looking him dead in the eye from beneath a clump of brush was a mangled face that he didn't recognize. The shiny blood-spattered badge lying nearby was enough to identify the man as Curt Bell. The antibodies had obviously regarded the ranger as a threat because of the things he allowed to go on in the forest. After all, it was his willingness to look the other way that brought about so much of nature's destruction.

Everett howled and jerked his leg free of the corpse's grasp. He was on his feet in seconds and running for the old green Ford. That would be his salvation. He found out just how wrong he was, however, when he made it to the truck and discovered it was locked. Groaning, he remembered seeing the keys lying near Jeff's remains.

The antibodies walked slowly toward him. They were in no rush. He would not make it out alive.

In those last few seconds, Everett thought about the nature of cancer and how the body rushed to amass defenses to protect itself. Sometimes, like in his daughter's case, the body was weak. Other times, like now, the body was stronger than the germs that invaded it. Why couldn't it be the other way around? Why couldn't his daughter be the strong one? The natural order of things wasn't always fair.

He was suddenly enraged at the way things worked. His daughter didn't deserve to die any more than the bear or the lumberjacks did. Yes, maybe Jeff deserved to die. Maybe he did too for all the things he had killed. But his daughter did not. He could imagine her lying there in that sterile hospital room while millions of rampant cells ravaged her body and fed off her health. The thought was impetus enough for action.

Everett rifled through his vest pockets until he found a cigarette lighter. The cap on the Ford's gas tank was of the antiquated variety. Once removed, Everett would have no trouble dropping the lighter down into the belly of the beast.

It was quite possible that his daughter would beat the cancer. But it was equally possible that she wouldn't. If she couldn't stop the ravages of nature, then what made this place any different? Why should it overcome disease when she could not?

Everett made his decision in a split second and sparked the flints until a flame appeared at the top of the lighter. He calmly dropped the lighter into the gas tank and waited for the destruction that would follow.

The antibodies rushed at him in those last fated seconds. Everett welcomed them with open arms.

"The cancer's waitin', boys," he said with a smile.

The heat blossomed from the belly of the Ford, engulfing Everett, the antibodies, and a portion of the surrounding forest. And like cancer, it just kept spreading.

The Thief, An Interlude

Max slammed the glass eye down on the floor and scurried away from it, gasping for breath. He had heard the stories about the big fire that ravaged nearly half of Easthaven Forest back in the summer of '95, but the cause of the fire had always been open to speculation. He was pretty sure he knew what had happened now. Still, it all seemed so surreal that he had gotten such information from a cursed glass eye and a piece of pine bark covered with... what? He frantically rubbed his hands against his pants, thinking the oily black substance on the bark might have been part of one of those things from the forest.

He could barely believe what he had seen, and yet he knew the stories about Magnusson's Eye were true. It did exactly what people claimed it did. It showed him a vision of those creatures from Easthaven Forest. The level of detail from the scene assured him that the vision was a true one and not simply the product of his overactive imagination.

But those things in the vision... surely, they couldn't be real. Could they? To accept such a presumption was to question the very nature of the world around him. Those weren't flesh and blood threats. Those things were part of a supernatural reality he wasn't quite ready to accept. Maybe there was a perfectly good explanation for it all. He just couldn't come up with one at the moment.

His mind raced at the thought of what other images he might see if he picked up the glass eye again and focused on one of the other items from the shadow box.

Max took a deep breath, glanced around the museum to make sure he was still alone, grabbed the glass eye off the floor, and chose another monster relic. This time he picked a tuft of hair from the shadow box. A tiny card beneath the clipping identified it as "Old Ezra." Max had no idea what that meant, but he gripped the hair in one hand and the eye in the other, relaxing his thoughts enough that his mind's eye opened. Immediately, a whole new world bloomed before him in a kaleidoscope of sight and sound.

Unable to look away, he watched that story unfold as well as the one after and the one after that...

What will you experience?

These are the things that Max Garfield, master thief and nighttime patron of Museum Nocturnus, saw when he held Magnusson's Eye.

Old Ezra

It all seemed to happen in slow motion, reminding Pritchard of something he'd once seen on the Discovery Channel. Like crocodiles, they sat there, unmoving yet alert, camouflaged by a heavy thicket of bushes and trees, waiting on an Impala or a Jaguar to race by. Pritchard's Mustang wasn't nearly that sleek of a beast, but he knew that the troopers wouldn't hesitate to pull him over since he was doing nearly eighty in a fifty-five. Which meant he was either going to have to outrun them or get caught with several little baggies full of marijuana in the trunk.

It was strange to see so many patrol cars out here in the middle of nowhere, and it was totally unexpected. Pritchard had decided on this route because the road was largely untraveled and in severe need of extensive repair in several spots. Given the nature of the cargo he was hauling in his trunk, he needed to minimize all contact with law enforcement, and he had reasoned that this route would be the best way to transport the drugs without getting caught. Yet judging by the phalanx of troopers that were waiting on him, silent and menacing, he had done exactly the opposite and found every patrol car in a fifty-mile radius. Besides them, however, Pritchard hadn't seen another vehicle for the past hour. It was just the sort of luck he was used to.

Pritchard stared at the legion of Crown Victorias as he flew by and waited on one of them to flash their lights and pull out. One of the souped-up patrol cars inched forward a little as if debating the merits of a pursuit. Pritchard gripped the steering wheel tightly and prayed to God that he wouldn't see flashing lights in his rearview mirror. He didn't, but that was only because the trooper didn't turn them on. Instead, he eased onto the highway, a ravenous crocodile gliding into black water. Like animals responding to the scent of blood, the other cars slowly followed, and Pritchard knew that he was in deep trouble.

The first trooper shot past him like a bottle rocket, and he almost thought that they were going to leave him alone. But then the car pulled in front of him, a matching bookend to the one that had swerved in behind, and he knew that this was probably going to be painful. The other four patrol cruisers came up fast in the left lane, leaving him nowhere else to go but the shoulder of the road. Reluctantly, he pulled over, praying that they would just write him a citation for exceeding the speed limit and let him go on his merry way. Of course, it never worked out that nicely. Pritchard knew. He had been through this routine far too many times to hold out that much hope.

Only one of the officers stepped out of his car. It was the one who had pulled in behind him. Staring nervously in the rearview mirror, Pritchard could see the patrolman's thick, muscled forearms swinging at his sides, brushing against his revolver every now and then. There was no sign of a billy club. Ordinarily, that would have brightened Pritchard's day. In this case, however, it simply meant that the officer would have to shoot him if he got rowdy. Pritchard took a deep breath and put his hands on the steering wheel so the patrolman could see he wasn't loading a pistol or reaching behind the seat for a hunting knife. Above all else, he was determined to cooperate.

The patrolman rapped on the glass twice, and Pritchard quickly rolled his window down.

"Get out of the car," the patrolman said sternly, his jaw flexing with each word. "And don't open your mouth. I don't want to cut you just yet."

Pritchard hadn't seen the knife at first glance, but he certainly saw it now, gleaming in the dusky sunlight, strapped to the officer's right thigh. He immediately recognized the blade as the kind that hunters usually took with them to field dress their kills. Understandably, the thought of being flayed and disemboweled by some deranged highway patrolman scared him to death, but he was determined to do exactly as he was told. Pritchard opened the door slowly and started to step out just like he had been instructed to when the trooper grabbed him by the shirt collar and threw him from the car.

Pritchard kissed the pavement and could taste fresh warm blood trickling from his nose and lips. Apparently not satisfied with the amount of pain he had doled out, the patrolman rammed his boot down hard into Pritchard's back. It was all Pritchard could do not to scream. And if that wasn't bad enough, he could hear the squeaking of doors being opened, and the heavy thud of doors being shut as the rest of the troopers stepped out of their cars.

"Oh great," Pritchard thought to himself, envisioning a throng of crocodiles converging on a fallen zebra like he'd seen dozens of times before on those nature programs. "Now they're really going to have some fun with me."

"Do you think he'll be enough, Gordon?" one of the troopers asked gruffly.

"I 'spect so," Gordon replied. Although Pritchard couldn't look up with a boot pressed into the small of his back, he could tell by the voice that Gordon was the man who had thrown him from the car and was currently holding him down. "Jackson, did those other knuckleheads set up the roadblocks like I told 'em to?"

"Yeah, we radioed them when you got out of the car," Jackson replied. "As far as I can tell, we've got this whole stretch of highway to ourselves. They're detouring everybody through to Mingus County. So, this part of Thornmire County should be free and clear."

Pritchard tensed at the mention of roadblocks. Things had happened too quickly for him to realize that he hadn't heard the first passing car. Yet now that he noticed the silence and understood why there weren't automobiles rumbling up and down the blacktop, he grew nervous at the thought that no one would be able to hear him if he screamed.

"Old Ezra ought to like this one," Jackson said with a wry smirk on his face. "Are we sure that nobody's going to come looking for him?"

"Yeah," Gordon said over a mouthful of something. "I ran his license plate and found out that he's done some small-time drug running. He's done a little time in the pen too, and is on parole. People like him aren't missed. In fact, it's usually a surprise when they show up alive. And I wouldn't worry about anybody hunting for this one. I doubt anybody cares enough to put forth that much effort."

Pritchard heard Gordon spit and felt something hot and wet land on the back of his neck. It wasn't much of a stretch to assume that it was tobacco juice. Pritchard could hear the other men laughing at his humiliation. He grunted as the thick brown spittle ran down his skin.

"You got something to say down there, boy?" Gordon asked over the chew of Red Man that was tucked safely away in his cheek. Pritchard shook his head, unwilling to speak. He hadn't made a move so far to defend himself or even argue about the treatment he was receiving, but that didn't mean he wasn't going to. He simply had to wait for the right moment.

"I didn't think so," Gordon said harshly. "That offer to cut you with my knife still stands."

Pritchard had been in situations like this enough times to know that Gordon was just itching for him to say something. Which is exactly why he didn't.

"Okay, boys," Gordon continued, unperturbed. "Here's how we're going to play this one. The roads are blocked, so we don't have to worry about anybody driving by and videoing the whole thing. That means we can take our time and do this right. Richardson, I want you and Clavell to patrol the strip of highway that we've got blocked off just in case somebody manages to slip through. Martin, you and Borland are going to stand watch in front of the trail. Jackson and I are going to take Mr. Raymond Pritchard down to meet Old Ezra, introduce him properly. Everybody, keep your walkies on just in case I need a word with you. As far as I can tell, though, this should be a fairly smooth operation. Does everybody understand what they're supposed to do?"

Pritchard's face was still ground into the pavement, bits of glass and sharp gravel biting into his cheek, so he couldn't see any of the other men's faces. But his hearing was still in perfect working order, and he only heard four out of the five men respond to Gordon's question. Gordon must have heard it too.

"Borland, you got what I'm saying? You're not exactly filling me with confidence here."

"I understand," Borland said cautiously. Although Pritchard had only spent the better part of five minutes with Gordon, he knew that Borland's answer wasn't going to prove satisfactory.

"Somehow," Gordon replied slowly, "I'm not really sure I believe you. Now, I realize that this is your first time in for something like this, and you may not understand just how important your job is, but we can't have you turning heel on us. There's too much at stake here."

"I just don't want to get caught," Borland said softly, obviously afraid of Gordon. "Somebody might see us, and then we would have a lot of explaining to do. I've got a wife and three kids to feed. I can't do that very well from prison."

"You just haven't been one of the gang long enough," Gordon reasoned. "Or you would know that there's nothing to worry about. First off, we're the law around here. Nobody tells us what to do. Second, just about the only people that use this road anymore are the farmers when they're driving their tractors to the fields. Everybody else takes the highway. It's a lot quicker. Besides that, we're going to have roadblocks set up if someone should happen to come in this direction. But I can promise you that they won't. Honestly, I don't know how much simpler I can make it. All you have to do is what I say. Everything else will fall into place."

"And Gordon knows what he's talking about," Pritchard blurted out before he could catch himself. Gordon's boot pressed hard into his spine, threatening to grind every vertebra into chalky white dust. One moment, it seemed as though the burly patrolman had shifted every bit of his weight onto that one foot. The next, Pritchard felt the boot leave his back completely. But it wasn't much of a relief. Gordon's knife was at Pritchard's throat before he could even think about making a run for it. The sharp edge scraped at his skin like a barber's straight razor, and he could feel a thin trickle of blood running down his chest, mingling with the tobacco spit that had found its way around to the front of his shirt.

"You're not very smart, boy," Gordon said firmly, pulling Pritchard's head back enough that they could nearly meet each other's gaze. "Don't count on making a liar out of me. I'll do what I say. You won't get but one chance to find that out."

"I'd do what he says," Borland said meekly as if he had experienced Gordon's wrath first-hand. "This ain't no game."

"I'm glad to hear you say that, Borland," Gordon interjected. "It makes me feel a little bit better about sending you out. Makes me feel like I can trust you. And that's something that I can't say about most men. You'll do fine. I'm sure. You're just a little green at this sort of thing. But you'll get used to it in time. Besides, it's not like this is something we do every day. A few times a year is all it takes, and Old Ezra is happy. Now, help me get this boy to his feet. We gotta get this thing moving. People will start to complain if they're held up too long."

With a little help from Gordon, Pritchard stood up like a man who has had more than his fair share of drink. Gordon waved his hand once, and the men set off on their assigned duties. Jackson, however, stayed put, his gun pressed hard into Pritchard's back like an accusing finger. It was the same spot that Gordon had mistaken for a footrest. Pritchard wanted to complain about the sharp, spider-webbing pains that spread from his back out toward his abdomen and ribs, but somehow, he felt like these men were anything but sympathetic.

Like good Boy Scouts, the three of them started off into the woods, Gordon out in front, Jackson bringing up the rear. The best Pritchard could tell, there wasn't any sort of trail. Not at first, anyway. Gradually, however, a small path of dirt began to tunnel through the thick carpet of pine needles like Egyptians through Red Sea waters. Somehow, Pritchard couldn't stretch the comparison to include Gordon as some Cecil B. DeMille-era Moses. That would have been a bit much.

Up until now, Pritchard had gone along with everything that was said, thinking that his willing participation might gain him some points with the troopers. That was no longer the case. Fairly certain that he was going to die anyway, he was no longer quite so concerned about going along with the plan. Or about keeping quiet.

"Where are we going?" he asked, fully aware that these two were probably dragging him out in the middle of nowhere to torture him and put a bullet in his skull.

"To meet Old Ezra," Gordon said calmly right before his hand caught Pritchard across the left cheek. "We've got a lot of local towns to think about here. Honest, hard-working men who don't need any trouble. Men like you are the answer to that problem."

"You full of wisdom, Master Yoda," Pritchard replied with a choppy accent, wincing in expectation of the coming pain. "You have evy-ting figured out." Surprisingly enough, Gordon didn't retaliate. He was too busy trying to navigate his way through a maze of snaking, gnarled roots that jutted from the earth like zealous fingers that might grab him at any second.

"I've got a lot of money, you know?" Pritchard said, throwing out any lie that might buy him a little time. "The old hash is pretty profitable if you don't get caught. I could make it worth your while to let me go."

At the mention of money, the pistol barrel that had been firmly pressed into Pritchard's back eased up a little.

"We don't need your money," Gordon was quick to say as he bounded over a fallen tree that looked as though it had been struck by lightning. "Ain't that right, Jackson?"

"Well," Jackson said noncommittally. Gordon stopped the processional and turned to look at the man who was supposed to be guarding his back.

"Well, what?"

"Well, this job don't exactly pay for the risk that's involved. And I could use some extra cash. Maybe we should let this one go and find another."

Gordon arched one eyebrow and shifted the tobacco from one cheek to the other.

"Now look here, Jackson, this ain't a matter of money. This is about helping the poor people who can't help themselves. If we don't take care of this, Old Ezra will ruin every family in Thornmire County. Besides, I'll let you in on a little secret. And you won't tell any of the other boys about it. The farmers have been chipping in a little for our trouble. I'll cut you in on it. Maybe that will help out some."

"You've been holding out," Jackson said, flabbergasted.

"A little," Gordon confessed. "But I'll make it right. You just don't worry about that."

"You better make it more than right," Jackson growled through clenched teeth, ramming the gun back into Pritchard's kidneys.

"The offer still stands, Jackson," he whispered as the pain in his lower back eased up. "You can think about it while we walk."

Branches crackled underfoot, and dust motes floated through the greenish haze of forest dusk like bits of flesh suspended in formaldehyde. It seemed like the perfect setting for a torturous death, and Pritchard's mind scrambled for some method of escape. In the distance, however, something was shrieking in the shadows, providing the eerie soundtrack to the movie of Pritchard's demise.

"What was that?" he asked calmly, trying to hold the panic at bay.

"Old Ezra," Jackson said cautiously. "But you'll meet him soon enough. Most of the people we bring out here aren't nearly as anxious to be introduced to him as you are, though."

Up until now, Pritchard had assumed that Old Ezra was some aging hermit out here in the forest who looked the other way while the troopers beat their prisoners senselessly. But he had never heard a sound like that come from any other human being before.

"We're not sure where he came from," Jackson explained, all too familiar with the slight tremble in Pritchard's voice. "All we know is that if we don't make him happy, he'll take what he wants from the nearby farms. And that hasn't turned out so well in the past."

"The Jacobs family lost two daughters to Old Ezra," Gordon added. "The Matthews boy lost an arm and an eye. Jenkins lost about ten head of cattle. Just about every family around has lost a dog or a cat. And Jackson, well... I'll just let Jackson show you himself."

Gordon stopped long enough for Jackson to pull one leg of his trousers up. Pritchard's eyes widened a little at the sight of the prosthetic.

"Took my leg off at mid-thigh, he did. I think I've learned to walk pretty well with this fake. But that don't make up for what I lost. I almost didn't pass the physical because of what Ezra did to me. Luckily, Gordon has a lot of influence with some of the guys at the top."

Pritchard stared stupidly at Gordon, waiting for some further explanation.

"Old Ezra isn't really selective when it comes to that sort of thing," Gordon said almost cheerfully. "I guess you can see why the farmers are all so concerned about keeping him happy."

No matter how hard he tried, Pritchard couldn't conjure up the image of the thing that was screaming like a child dipped in hot tar. Fortunately, it was just about dark beneath the forest's canopy, save for a stray beam of weak sunlight here and there. That didn't keep Pritchard, however, from hearing the chains rattle and clang together in the darkness like something out of a medieval dungeon. It was almost as if someone were banging two lengths of heavy gauge pipe together. Which meant that the chain was obviously very, very thick and attached to something very, very big. The thought wasn't very reassuring.

"You chained him up?" Pritchard asked.

"We tried, didn't we, Jackson?" Gordon replied, pushing through the overgrowth like a soldier in the bush.

"Yeah, we tried. And even now, I'm not sure how ol' Jack Manchester and his boys managed to get chains on both of Old Ezra's... well, I guess you might call 'em arms. They had found a couple of good-sized oaks not too far from here and hooked the chains up to them. I guess they figured if the thing was tied to trees that big with chains that strong, it would be okay. Problem solved. Only it wasn't."

"Old Ezra snapped those chains like little strands of thread and went right on about his business," Gordon added, stopping long enough to roll up his shirt sleeve to reveal a long, snaking scar running almost the entire length of his arm. "Unfortunately, his business was us."

"That's right," Jackson said, motioning to his prosthetic leg. "Of course, we got off easy. All three of the Manchesters looked like hamburger meat on a butcher's shop floor after that, and we had to rake up what was left of 'em and carry 'em back in garbage bags. Nobody's bothered trying to take the chains off Old Ezra since then. As a matter of fact, it gives you a little warning before you actually run up on him. You can hear the chains jingling. And believe me, where Old Ezra's concerned, you want to know exactly where he is."

"Why didn't you just shoot him?" Pritchard asked.

"You ever try shooting into a brick wall, boy?" Gordon asked him as he pushed a heavy branch away from his face, letting it go just in time to slap Pritchard across the mouth. "If you haven't, I'll just tell you that it doesn't work too well. And Old Ezra's every bit as durable and steadfast as a wall. He's got skin that's as tough as sheet metal to boot. Which means the bullets don't faze him much. Still, bullets were all that saved us on that day that Manchester and his sons bit the dust. They bought us enough time to get out of there. I wouldn't want to try something like that again."

In the growing darkness, Pritchard nearly ran into Gordon's back as the big man stopped abruptly. Jackson inhaled sharply, obviously aware that they were close. A musty breeze that stank of dead animals, blood, decay, moldy plants, and the faintest traces of human excrement blew gently, rustling the leaves on the trees and the hair on Pritchard's head. It nearly made Pritchard sick.

The trail they had been following ran into a bleak clearing, illuminated by thin, sick rays of wan moonlight. The dark mouth of a small cave could barely be seen at the end of the open field. Pritchard couldn't help but gasp at the mounds of bones that were piled up like last week's garbage outside the entrance to the cave.

"You'd better get used to the idea of all these dead parts lying around, Pritchard," Gordon said with no small amount of mirth. "You'll be just another heap of 'em in another hour or so."

"You guys are serious?" Pritchard said, his voice a soft whimper in the dark. Until now, he had managed to convince himself that he might actually walk out of this alive. Battered, beaten, bruised, and bloody. But alive. The sight of all the human remains sort of squashed that notion.

"We never meant for things to work out like this," Jackson said almost apologetically. "But we really didn't have any choice. It was Gordon's idea to lure Old Ezra into Sutter's Cavern in the first place. And that meant having bait. We tried heads of cattle, a couple of sows, a dozen chickens, just about any sort of animal that you could think of to get Old Ezra on the scent. But he didn't respond to anything but human blood. Gordon rounded up a couple of the local drunks when they were too plastered to care and brought them out here. After that, Old Ezra went into the cave willingly enough. The drunks never came out at all."

"Old Ezra hasn't been out again either," Gordon said a little more quietly than was his custom. "Of course, we keep him well fed."

"The town's own personal house pet," Pritchard said sarcastically. "How precious."

"Get a move on, Pritchard," Gordon growled, stepping into the mouth of the immense rock. "I'm tired of your lip. We'll see if Old Ezra can't take care of that little problem."

Inside the cave, the rattle of chains was nearly deafening. Thin trickles of water etched tiny fissures into the rock, and small, red salamanders scurried along the wet stone, looking for moist, dark hiding places. Listening to Old Ezra's screaming and shrieking, Pritchard thought to himself that finding a moist, dark hiding place of his own wasn't such a bad idea. Gordon must have thought so too. His purposeful, steady gait quickly became one of caution and deliberation once the long, winding tunnel stopped and the mouth of the cave opened up onto an enormous, black cavern.

"We're here!" Gordon shouted, struggling to make his voice heard above the cacophony of screeching metal and howling. Old Ezra growled at the prospect of company.

Because it was dark, Pritchard couldn't get a very good look at the beast at first. But what he saw was more than enough—a flash of fang, a gleam of claw, a dull burning eye like a smoldering ember of coal. Gordon was breathing much faster than normal, and Pritchard was glad to see that he wasn't quite as tough as he made out.

"Come on, Pritchard," Gordon said gruffly over his shoulder. "It's time to say goodbye."

"That offer about the payoff still stands, Jackson," Pritchard said over his shoulder as Gordon took a step forward. Jackson moved the gun barrel away from

Pritchard's kidneys, still bitter about the way Gordon had been holding out on him. Not wasting any time, Pritchard gave Gordon a shove from behind and listened to the big man wail like a heartsick widow as he rushed headlong into Old Ezra's waiting arms.

"Jackson!" Gordon howled, matching Old Ezra's wailing in an eerie off-key duet.

Although he wasn't sure of much, Pritchard could have sworn that he heard Gordon's bones crackling like dry wood in a fireplace.

Jackson had obviously never liked Gordon, and he quickly switched on his flashlight to watch the systematic destruction of the man who had indirectly cost him his leg by forcing him to go hunting with the other deputies. Pritchard screamed right along with Gordon at the sight of the thing that held him tight in its enormous grasp.

It looked like something that hell had regurgitated-vaguely reminding Pritchard of old renderings of the Greek Minotaur from the Labyrinth—with curved black horns jutting back from its forehead and stiletto claws tearing fiercely at what was left of Gordon. The beast was covered with dark, leathery skin, and just looking at that thick hide was enough to tell Pritchard that bullets wouldn't work. Gordon had apparently forgotten that little lesson as he was frantically trying to get to his gun.

With a scream, Old Ezra rammed one clawed fist through Gordon's midsection and held him high above its head, letting the blood from the erstwhile patrolman's mouth drip down into its own hideous, saw-toothed maw.

Crimson rivulets ran down both sides of the monster's mouth, splashing onto the floor of the cave, and it wouldn't have surprised Pritchard a bit to see the beast get down on all fours and lap at the blood like an animal at a clear, cool stream. As it was, there was still a little life left in Gordon, which meant that Old Ezra wasn't done with him yet. Gordon screamed once more as the beast wrapped him up in a lover's embrace and crushed the life out of him, gnawing at his head with those sharp, pointy teeth. Crocodile teeth, Pritchard thought right before Jackson dropped his flashlight in shock.

Pritchard knew that this was his one chance and made his move instantaneously. He had Jackson's .357 out of its holster before the highway patrolman could begin to register what had just happened.

"Let's go, Jackson," Pritchard said, trying hard to keep the tremor out of his voice. "I don't think you want to wait around for that thing to get finished with Gordon. Now move your butt back the way we came. And give me that walkie-talkie."

With Jackson leading the way, both men ran toward the mouth of the cave, panting and winded and scared for their lives as the clanging of chains announced the coming of Old Ezra like a fanfare of trumpets would have signaled the processional of a king. Although he hadn't planned on doing anything other than fleeing for his life at first, an idea crept into Pritchard's head as they neared the opening, and the more he thought about it, the more it seemed like the right thing to do.

As it was, Jackson was the first to reach the dark clearing littered with the bones of those that Gordon had brought down here as an appeasement to Old Ezra. Pritchard stopped right beside him and rammed the gun barrel into the patrolman's stomach.

"Sorry about this," Pritchard said as he pulled the trigger. Immediately, Jackson went down like a mob informant with both feet encased in concrete. Blood trickled through his fingers as he tried to stanch the flow with his hands.

"I don't guess you'll be needing this anymore," Pritchard said, pulling a handkerchief out of Jackson's back pocket and soaking up blood until the rag dripped a steady stream of viscous red. Jackson looked at him, more confused than anything else, and Pritchard left him there like that with the knowledge that soon he and Gordon would be together again.

From what little he knew about the monster, he was sure it wouldn't pass up fresh blood. His suspicions were confirmed a few moments later when he heard Jackson scream. Of course, he didn't feel bad about that one little bit, given the way Gordon and his boys had been running things. There was no telling how many innocent victims had passed through the nearby towns only to be stopped by this troupe of charlatan peace officers. Hopefully, that was all about to change.

Pritchard pulled Jackson's walkie-talkie off his belt as he ran and thumbed the button that would send his voice to those at the roadblock. He hoped he would sound enough like Gordon to get some response.

"I need everybody at the head of the path now," Pritchard said in his best southern drawl. "We've got ourselves a little problem here, boys, and Jackson and I need all the help we can get. That means you boys at the roadblock too. Get down here. Pronto!"

"We're on our way, boss," one of the patrolmen said quickly from the other end. "You and Jackson just hold tight."

Pritchard smiled at the thought that his little plan just might work and ran for his life through the ever-darkening forest.

The blood dripped copiously from the handkerchief as Pritchard ran back along the path toward the other patrolmen, and he made no attempt whatsoever to stanch the steady drizzle that marked the autumn leaves in spatters of red. Branches slapped him in the face like jealous women. Briars tore at his skin and clothing. He almost twisted his ankle when he jumped over a fallen tree. But he wasn't about to stop with Old Ezra hot on his heels. It was only when he got to the end of the trail and heard the reassurance of police sirens that he tossed the handkerchief toward the sound of the patrolmen and scurried off in the opposite direction.

"Are you there, boys?" Pritchard whispered from a heavy thicket of brush, fairly certain that Old Ezra would follow the scent of blood rather than the sound of his voice. The walkie-talkie crackled and popped, and

Pritchard quickly shoved it under his shirt to muffle the noise.

"We're here, Gordo," somebody replied through the cloth of Pritchard's torn shirt. "Our guns are drawn." That was all Pritchard needed to hear before turning the radio off.

From the sound of things, Old Ezra wasn't wasting any time pushing through the undergrowth to get to the blood. Thick branches snapped with gunshot reports. Leaves crackled loudly like bones breaking over and over again. The rustle of holly and jasmine was a deafening clamor, like the whoosh of the ocean that roars when listening to a conch shell. Pritchard's blood turned to ice when he heard the pop and snap of cracked branches get louder. But then Old Ezra evidently picked up on the scent again because the heavy thud of footsteps receded.

And then the screaming started.

The report of gunfire was like an ominous thunder, and the painful howling, a dark melody to a psychotic symphony. Pritchard was just starting to wonder if Gordon had been right about the effect of bullets on the creature when one by one, the guns stopped firing. The cessation of noise was like a dismal countdown to eradication, and the silence that followed was more ominous and foreboding than the screaming. Old Ezra shrieked like a banshee, and the chill that ran over Pritchard's skin was akin to a high-centigrade fever. He shivered visibly as the crunch and smack of bones being torn from flesh drifted through the dusky woods, a macabre counterpoint to the howling of moments before. It was all Pritchard could do to remain quietly in that one spot while Old Ezra had his fill, but eventually, the smacking of black lips stopped and the rustle of leaves grew louder as the beast headed back through the woods.

Pritchard didn't move for at least ten minutes after that, and when he did, his joints popped like corks from a dozen champagne bottles. Hesitantly, he headed toward the beginning of the trail and promptly threw up when he saw limbs scattered about the stretch of highway like roadkill. The patrol cars were parked on both sides of the road, and a few of them still had their lights flashing. But the emergency was over. Wearily, Pritchard picked one of the Crown Victorias at random and was delighted to find that the keys were still in the ignition. He wasn't sure he could have scavenged through body parts until he found a set. That would have simply been too much.

With a sigh, he opened the door and flipped on the police-band radio that was mounted to the dash.

"County mounty, this is Gordo, here," Pritchard said wearily. "We've got a little bit of trouble down at the path. Send help immediately. Old Ezra's in a mighty fierce mood today."

And with that, he hung up and got in his Mustang, no longer worried about Gordon, the marijuana in his trunk, or the deserted roadblock. With a certain sense of satisfaction, Pritchard couldn't help but think that sometimes the zebra escaped, and the crocodiles were left with their jaws open and their stomachs empty. And sometimes, there were things even worse than the crocodiles. Pritchard couldn't wait until the beasts found that out.

Intermission

When the vision abated, Max discovered that he was drenched in sweat. He patted his shirt pockets unconsciously looking for a pack of cigarettes despite the fact that he had quit smoking more than twenty years ago. His body, however, hadn't forgotten the need for nicotine when the stress level got too high.

"Get a grip, Max," he said to himself, running a hand through his wiry hair. "You're acting like a scared child. They're just visions. Little more than movies in your mind."

But were his reactions unreasonable? Magnusson's Eye could catch glimpses of the hidden details of any item the owner possessed. Magnusson, being a hunter, had used the eye to suss out details about the strange and mythical creatures he wanted to capture. That didn't mean creatures were the only things about which the eye could provide details.

His thoughts, however, were all over the place at this point, and he didn't pursue the line of thinking any further.

"Let's use logic, Maxwell," the thief said to himself. "Reason it out. You're a smart guy."

What he had just seen was too much to comprehend. It felt real, but the more he thought about it, the more he realized that there was no way what he had just seen was actual. Was it a hallucination? Was he having a stroke? Monsters weren't real. Valley Falls was the strangest place he had ever lived, but even in a place like that, there were limits to the weirdness.

None of this made sense. Then again, nothing in a place like this was supposed to make sense, was it? He had broken into a museum filled with haunted and cursed items. What had he expected?

He paced around the room for a moment, pondering what to do. The next question that was poised on his lips was a valid one. "Do I keep going? Do I use the eye to see more? Maybe if I go a little further, I'll get a better understanding of the eye and what it really does."

So far, no harm had been done. What if the next vision could be used to help someone or save lives? Maybe Magnusson had tracked down the sorts of creatures from these visions for that very reason. If the visions were true, then killing those monsters would be a way of keeping the people of Valley Falls safe. Those black oily antibody creatures had killed more than their share of people. Old Ezra too.

"It would be irresponsible not to watch another," Max said with a smirk. "I could be a hero with knowledge learned from one of these."

Yet, even as he talked himself into grabbing the glass eye again, he knew he was lying to himself about his reasons for moving forward. He wasn't doing this for the public good. He was doing this to benefit himself in the hopes of learning something he could use to make a fortune.

"Maybe I could donate some of the fortune to charity," Max said, trying hard to convince himself that his motives weren't all selfish. In the back of his mind, however, he was trying hard to calculate just how much an actual Bigfoot might be worth.

Only once, and even then, only briefly, did he consider the fact that neither of the visions he had glimpsed so far had a pleasant outcome. These weren't Hallmark movies. It was likely the next story would be just as bloody and violent.

"Only one way to find out," Max said as he selected another item from the shadow box and relaxed his mind to allow the glass eye to work.

Strangely, the moment he closed his eyes, he could hear the sound of gospel singing.

Running Toward Eden

The church was a quaint white building with a nice green lawn. It had the customary stained-glass windows depicting the miracles of Christ, a small metal cross atop the steeple, and a gravel parking lot filled with assorted pickup trucks, dirty station wagons, and the standard fare of minivans. Organ music filtered from the open doors like warmth from an oven.

A drooping apple tree knelt in the church's front yard like a sinner searching for redemption. Bruised and rotten fruit dotted the ground, waiting for the birds to eat their fill. A little blonde girl sat on the steps with a bushel of apples from the tree, rolling them down slowly one at a time. Something was wrong with her. A small unkempt cemetery flanked the sanctuary. A few of the graves were adorned with silk flowers. Most hadn't been attended to in years and were covered with weeds.

All in all, it was a typical church, a thumbnail sketch that could have come from any of a dozen states in the Deep South. The only thing that wasn't typical of the scene was the fenced-in corral behind the church and the cages.

Nobody really seemed to pay the corral much attention. They all knew what it was for, what it held. To them, it simply contained another facet of their religion, just as the cups they used for the Lord's Supper contained the symbolic blood of Christ. The symbolism, however, ended with the grape juice that filled those cups. What lived inside those cages behind the church was real. It was the source of true miracles.

And a miracle, after all, was the one reason they came to the Church of the Crucified Nazarene in the first place.

The crippled staggered up to the church, bracing themselves with crutches. The sick hobbled in, supported by members of their families. The blind walked uncertainly, hoping that the steps leading up to the sanctuary hadn't moved since the last time they came to be healed. Despite their infirmities, the needy all wore their masks of hope. For many of them, this was their last chance.

"You're nervous," Becca said, clutching Connor's hand for reassurance.

"Why wouldn't I be?" Connor said, pulling away. "I know what kind of things go on here." Without thinking about it, he massaged the lump in his cheek. At one time, the lump could have easily been a wad of tobacco. Not anymore. Now it wasn't just something he could spit out and forget.

"This is going to work. I promise," Becca said. "And I know this isn't the most conventional way to do things, but keep an open mind about it." Although it was clear by the look on her face that she was optimistic, the words themselves held just a little too much false hope for Connor's liking.

He watched the parade of freaks march up the steps to the church and wondered if they were just as deluded as Becca. Surely, they all didn't think that God was going to miraculously heal them.

"I don't think I want to do this after all," Connor said as they started up the steps.

"This is a church of faith," Becca reminded him. "I've seen things here that you wouldn't believe. God can take that cancer away if you'll just let Him."

"I'm not religious," Connor said. "Never have been. Why would I expect to waltz in here and be healed when there are devout believers who have spent years praying without result?"

"Because I have faith even when you don't."

"Places like this make me uncomfortable. I can't promise that I'm going to stick around once things get started. All those people shouting and clapping and speaking in tongues makes me feel weird."

"Well, having your cheek rot off could be a lot more uncomfortable. Don't you think?"

"I've got a question for you, since you've got all the answers," Connor said as they took a seat at the rear of the church. "If faith is the key to healing, why aren't you healed? You've still got all that scar tissue, and it doesn't seem to be going away. You may have all the faith in the world, but you still can't have children."

It was clear Becca didn't like the question but knew she had to answer. "God is not a genie who grants wishes," she said. "It's not that simple. Sometimes tests of faith aren't instantaneously rewarded. I'll be healed eventually. God won't let me down."

"I couldn't have said it any better myself," a booming voice said from behind them.

Connor turned and found himself staring at the tallest man he had ever seen. The man looked to be in his sixties with thinning white hair and deep-set eyes that looked like bits of coal. There was a certain electric intensity about him that made him seem like one of the old prophets from the Bible. Moses, perhaps. Or Abraham.

"So, this is the Connor I've heard so much about," the reverend observed. "Did he come to be healed? Or is he just curious about what we do here?"

"I've got cancer," Connor said. "In my jaw. I guess that's what too much tobacco will do for you. I've been chewing since I was thirteen."

"Be careful," Webster said. "Your sins will always find you out. The body is God's temple and should not be abused."

"I'm sure you haven't always been a saint," Connor said defensively.

"My sins aren't the ones in question here," Webster said. "You're the one whose transgressions have manifested themselves through affliction. But it doesn't matter. Whether you know it or not, you've come to the right place. Faith is what this church is built on, and soon the cages out back will be opened for your infirmity."

"Care to elaborate?"

"A doctor always goes to the source of an infection," Webster replied. "You wouldn't amputate an arm to save a leg, would you?"

"I don't understand what you mean," Connor confessed.

Reverend Webster smiled and shook his head knowingly. "Of course you don't. Let me try to put this in terms you can grasp. Man hasn't always sinned. There was a time in the beginning when humanity was perfect. This would be like a body being free of infection. Then the serpent tempted Eve, and the virus was released into the world. Your affliction is evidence that you've sinned. To rid you of the affliction, we go to the heart of the sin. We go to the tempter himself and beseech him to take the temptation away. With that goes the sin and the sickness."

"If you say so," Connor said, still puzzled.

Reverend Webster nodded and checked his watch. "You'll see in a few minutes," he said.

The chattering in the sanctuary was soon quieted by lush textured chords from an organ.

"Brothers and Sisters, I'm glad you're here," the reverend said from the pulpit. "But even more, God's glad you are here. He's happy for an opportunity to manifest His power and show you that He's the supreme authority over everything, including death. God is a merciful and all-powerful God. But He's also a bit picky. Sin is an abomination to The Father, and He refuses to look upon it. That's where the distance between you and Heaven comes from. That's also why you've come here today. To rid yourself of sin and the physical manifestations of it."

The room was a chorus of amens and hallelujahs set to the tune of "Victory in Jesus." Connor glanced over at the woman seated at the organ and thought to himself that she was probably the most normal looking person in the room. Then he noticed that she was missing both legs from the knees down.

"Is there a man among us who hasn't sinned?" Webster asked. "I think I can speak for every one of us when I say that we've all fallen short. Yet, sometimes, we take that for granted. We pass each other on the street and overlook the obvious afflictions that are outward manifestations of the wrongs we've committed. Sometimes it takes a newcomer to bring the truth full center again."

"No," Connor whispered as he realized what was coming.

"Take this young man, for instance," Reverend Webster said, pointing at Connor. "He was a slave to tobacco, and now he has a tumor on his jaw. Pretty sufficient reminder, if you ask me. But has God not promised us that there is a chance for redemption? Has He not given us sufficient means to erase the past? I say that He has."

On the reverend's cue, several rough-looking farmer-types in bib overalls stepped out the side door of the sanctuary. Connor instinctively knew where they were going.

The cages...

Until now, he had only guessed at what was being kept there, but the return of the farmers confirmed his every fear. The snakes writhed in their hands, eager to strike.

Connor didn't know much about snakes, but he knew enough to realize that they were poisonous and could very likely kill him with one bite.

"Since the beginning of time," the reverend said, "the serpent has personified evil. By placing our faith in God, we can overcome that evil and control the hold it has over our lives."

"I'm outta here," Connor said, rising up from the pew as one of the farmer-types held out a three-foot cottonmouth to him.

"Take it, brother," he said. "Show God how much you believe in Him."

"G-get away from me with that thing," Connor stammered. "I'm afraid of snakes."

"We're all afraid of something," Webster chimed in from the pulpit. "That's where having a strong set of beliefs comes in. Go ahead. Take the serpent. Grab evil by the throat. Trust that God will keep the snake from striking. That kind of faith is the only thing that will ever heal you."

"Please," Becca pleaded. "Take it, Connor. Do it for us."

Connor looked at Becca, saw the tears streaming down her face, and knew that she truly believed this was the way.

"I'm not doing this," he maintained. "I'm sorry."

Becca's face hardened. Her eyes went cold. "Fine," she said. "Your cancer. Not mine."

The fact that Connor had declined the serpents simply meant that there were more of them for the other fanatics in the congregation. The lady sitting behind them took a snake in each greedy hand and began to dance. Her eyes rolled back in her head, and the pins holding her tightly wrapped bun in place came loose, spilling her hair around her shoulders and down her curved back. The snakes squirmed in her tight-fisted grip.

Connor backed away from her. "Let's go," he told Becca.

"I'm not going anywhere," Becca said.

Connor sighed. "You're riding with me, and I'm leaving."

"I'll get a ride," Becca said.

"Fine," Connor said as he slipped out of the pew. "Suit yourself."

He barely got halfway down the aisle when two of the farmer-types that had helped bring in the snakes parked themselves in front of the doors. "You need God," one of them said. "And you're not leaving until you find Him."

"Let me out," Connor said.

"No," the other said, pulling a Buck knife out of his overalls. "Not until this is done."

Connor didn't want to start a fight that he knew he would lose. As calmly as he could manage under the circumstances, he found a seat on the back row and tried to quell his rising temper.

Soon everyone, Becca included, was handling snakes. The church was a frenzied house of flailing limbs, fluttering eyelids, and foreign tongues. The steady percussive sound of rattlers provided a subtle backbeat to all of the chanting and strange words that were floating through the air like the feathers of fallen angels. Connor kept checking the door to see if Reverend Webster's thugs were still there. They were.

"Brothers and Sisters!" Reverend Webster shouted from the pulpit. "We face evil every day in all its guises. Some of our trials are small and readily handled, like these serpents. Others aren't so small and require the force and prayers of a church like ours. Since the beginning of time, the world has been a battlefield of opposing forces. Good versus evil. God versus Satan. And why is this so? Why is this a problem for us? The answer is that we were born into sin. The root of our problem goes all the way back to the Garden of Eden where Eve was tempted."

"Our sins can control us," Webster continued. "Or we can control them. Our sins are like these snakes. We can release our grip on them and hope they won't be a problem any longer. That's the exact moment they will come back to bite us and doom us to eternal hell. Or we can be proactive and kill the evil in our lives before it has a chance to ruin us. Faith, of course, is the key."

The reverend motioned to one of his congregation, and the little girl with blonde ringlets joined Webster on stage. Webster kissed the little girl on the top of the head and made her face the crowd.

"No," Connor whispered.

"This is Virginia," Webster said as his congregation continued to dance and tempt fate. "She's been sick for a very, very long time. Was born that way, in fact. But I would venture to say that she has more faith than anyone in this room and triumphs daily because of it. Let her be an example to us all."

The little girl readily accepted two writhing cottonmouths and held them up for everyone to see.

"Ssssssssnakesssss," she said in a long, drawn-out voice.

Connor stood up with the intent of helping the little girl. "And what was her sin?" He felt two hands clamp down on his shoulders. The deacons glared at him and showed him their tobacco-stained teeth.

Realizing that he was a prisoner here in this church, Connor sat down and watched in horror as Virginia lost her grip on one of the cottonmouths. The serpent hissed and sank its fangs into her. It was only a matter of seconds before her eyelids fluttered, and she fell to the floor in the grip of a massive seizure.

"God won't let anything happen to her," Reverend Webster explained. "Our faith will guide her through."

"She needs to go to a hospital!" Connor shouted. His voice was buried beneath the din of so much shouting and praising.

"Hospitals," Webster said, spitting the word out. "Why are people so quick to dismiss God in times like these?"

"God invented common sense so we wouldn't pick up snakes that are poisonous," Connor said.

"Do you believe in God?"

Connor swallowed hard. He wasn't sure what kind of answer would be satisfactory here.

"I believe in a higher power, yes."

"But do you believe in God?"

"I'm not sure."

"Do you believe in Satan?"

"I believe that there is evil in the world."

"If I could prove to you that Satan exists, would that lead you to believe in God?"

Conner was nervous. He noticed men moving closer to his pew. He didn't know how to answer.

Webster smiled and motioned to his deacons. "Open the Penance Pit," he said.

"No," Becca said, snapping out of the trance-like state she'd been in. The snakes squirmed in her fists. "Don't put him in there."

"I'm trying to save your boyfriend's soul," Webster said.

Becca didn't seem quite so nailed to the cause anymore. She looked at Connor with tears in her eyes. It was enough to make him uneasy and a little scared.

The deacons did as they were told and began moving some of the pews around. Although he hadn't noticed it before, Connor realized that there was some sort of trap door set into the floor of the church.

"Don't worry," Webster said as one of the deacons raised the door to reveal a pit full of snakes. "I'll send Virginia in with you to protect you from Methuselah."

Connor started to run, but several men grabbed him and manhandled him toward the pit. It wasn't much of a fight, and he soon found himself cast into a room full of dark slithering shapes. As promised, Virginia was thrown in with him. She trembled and twitched as the snake's venom raced through her veins.

The last thing Connor saw before the door was closed was Becca peering over the edge at him and Webster's leering face.

Then darkness.

Connor tried to remain calm and keep his wits about him, but it was a difficult thing to manage with so many snakes slithering over his legs, up his arms, and across his chest. He wanted to scream so badly but refused to give Webster that sort of satisfaction. His only hope at this point was that Becca had finally come to her senses. Maybe she was going to get the police.

Amazingly enough, he hadn't been bitten by any snakes yet, but he knew that one wrong move could change that. Hesitantly, he reached out his hand, hoping that Virginia was nearby. He could hear her ragged breathing and knew that she wouldn't last long.

"Let me out!" Connor shouted. His voice was drowned out by a rousing rendition of "At the Cross".

Snakes hissed all around him, and Connor felt sure that one of them was about to strike as he reached out for

Virginia. Yet, he didn't feel the sting of fangs, only the tenderness of Virginia's skin. The skin was cold and clammy to the touch, still a little sticky from the apples. For a moment, he was certain that she was already dead. Then, she spoke to him.

"Methuselah will be here soon," she whispered to him in the darkness.

"We need to get out of here," Connor said.

"A serpent tricked us into sin. A serpent can take it away again," she said in singsong.

It took Connor a moment for the significance of that to truly sink in. "You mean that allowing yourself to be bitten by these serpents is your way of repentance."

"Methuselah can heal you."

"Who is Methuselah?" Connor asked.

But Virginia didn't reply. Instead, she lapsed back into unconsciousness.

Thin slats of meager light filtered in through the cracks in the door above them. Connor squinted and tried to get a better idea of his surroundings, but one of the pews was quickly shifted back into place, effectively blocking out what little illumination there was.

In those brief seconds before he was plunged into complete darkness, Connor had observed that a set of tunnels actually branched off from the Penance Pit, snaking off in different directions. He had absolutely no idea where any of them could lead but reasoned that one of them might offer some form of escape.

Thankful that he hadn't completely given up tobacco altogether, Connor pulled a lighter out of his pocket. He flicked the lighter and gasped at the moving, undulating mass of snakes that were squirming beneath his feet.

He gasped as he looked around for Virginia. Strangely enough, she seemed to have disappeared. He scanned the nearby tunnels for any sign of her. There was no possible way that she could have gotten up and staggered out of here in her condition. No doubt the cottonmouth's poison was already firmly entrenched in her system and debilitating her minute by minute.

There was no place else she could have gone. Unless…

Connor eyed the mass of snakes in front of him and caught a brief glimpse of white in their midst. Virginia had been wearing a white dress. The snakes moved around enough to show him another glimpse, this time of Virginia's pink skin.

The lighter went out, and Connor used the brief respite to gather his courage. This poor little girl couldn't climb out of her situation without help. Her parents had brought her here and forced her into this lifestyle, ignoring the dangers. And now she was covered in hundreds of venomous snakes and on her way to succumbing to the cottonmouth's bite.

"Faith," Connor said, spitting out the word like something rotten. This little girl had possessed faith, and look at where it had gotten her. Maybe Becca had gone through something similar as a child. Maybe that's why she didn't consider this bizarre or bent in any way.

Realizing what he had to do, Connor flicked his lighter again. Adders, racers, king and bull snakes slithered across his boots and each other. Connor shook his leg lightly to discourage one from crawling up the leg of his jeans. A rattler hissed at him, angry that it had been disturbed.

Carefully, Connor reached his hand into the working mass of serpents. The snakes parted for him, and he found Virginia's ankle easily enough. Snakes fell off the little girl like old scales as he hauled her out. Her skin was clammy and cold to the touch.

In the church above, the congregation was singing "Shall We Gather At the River".

The song made him think of water moccasins. He shuddered and tried to put the thought out of his mind. It was a difficult thing to do when he felt snakes slithering all around him.

Once Virginia was completely out from beneath the moving wave of serpentine flesh, Connor shook her slightly in case some of the filthy creatures had found their way into her clothing. A black racer and a dark brown snake with black stripes fell out of her dress. Satisfied that he had gotten rid of them all, Connor threw the little girl over his shoulder and took a close look at the tunnels, hoping to spot something that would tell him which way to go. A faint reddish glow emanated from one. Hoping that it was the last fading rays of the sun, Connor chose that direction and carefully tiptoed toward the tunnel.

Several snakes struck at him as he walked over, around, and sometimes on top of them. Their fangs were made harmless, however, by the steel-toed work boots that he wore. Knowing that his luck would eventually run out, Connor hurried into the tunnel, breathing a sigh of relief once he realized that there were no snakes this far up. Yet there was something that made him pause.

"It can't be," he said as he surveyed the enormous skin. It must have been twenty feet long and five feet wide. A snake would have to live a hundred lifetimes to grow this large. Methuselah, he remembered. The name would certainly fit.

Instinctively, he turned back toward one of the other tunnels only to find that a veritable army of snakes had fallen in behind them, blocking their way. Connor thought about chancing it but decided against it when a line of cobras rose up and began to spit venom in his direction.

Virginia shuddered in his arms.

"Just hang on a little bit longer," he said to the unconscious little girl. "We'll be out of here before you know it."

"The exit is this way," a husky voice whispered from the opposite end of the tunnel.

"Who's there?" Connor asked.

"A friend," the voice said. "I'll show you how to get out of here, but there's something I need from you first."

Connor knew this was a trick of some sort, but there was no other way out. He was stuck down here with the snakes and whatever or whoever this was.

"What's the deal?" he asked.

"Give me your sins," the voice instructed.

"I don't understand," Connor admitted.

"You obviously weren't listening to Reverend Webster when he explained the nature of sin and how it manifests itself in physical deformities and maladies."

"I heard it. I just didn't believe it."

"Come a little closer," the voice instructed. "You'll believe soon enough."

Connor flicked his lighter again and noticed that Virginia's eyes were rolling back in her head. He gritted his teeth in frustration. There was no other choice. He walked deeper into the tunnel, following the reddish glow.

"You've got what I need," the voice said.

"Who are you?" Connor asked.

"I'm known by many names," the voice whispered. "These people call me Methuselah."

"What should I call you?"

"How about Father?"

Although it was clear that the voice was devious and full of deceit, it was also alluring in a strange sort of way. It reminded Connor of stories he'd heard about sirens luring sailors to their deaths. This voice had that same magnetic quality to it.

He had already prepared himself for the fact that Methuselah was a snake, and a big one at that. What he hadn't prepared himself for was the origins of this particular creature. The serpent sat there at the end of the tunnel, coiled and alert, its eyes looking like rubies.

"Where did you come from?" Connor asked. "And how are you able to speak?"

"Where do any of us come from?" the serpent replied cryptically. "As for how I'm able to speak-think about it. I've been around a very long time."

"I'm not very good with riddles," Connor admitted.

"Maybe if I offered you an apple, you would realize who I am. Adam and Eve certainly would."

Connor gasped. "Impossible," he said.

"Not true," Methuselah responded. "Give me your sins, and I'll show you."

"Why do you want my sins?" Connor asked.

"It's what I live for," the serpent admitted. "Without sin, I would have no reason for existing and would die. It's why I tempted them in the first place. I needed to feed."

"Where does faith come in?" Connor asked, trying to play it cool even though he was panicking inside.

"I'll heal you and show you the way out."

"Are you Satan?"

The serpent laughed.

Methuselah opened his mouth to reveal a set of fangs as big as butcher knives.

Connor screamed, but it was too late to protest. The snake's fangs driving into Virginia's limp body and Methuselah's laughter were the last things he remembered in the cave. When he woke up, he found himself back in the church, surrounded by the curious. Becca was fanning him furiously with a hymnal.

"Are you okay?" she asked.

"Have you conquered your sins?" Reverend Webster asked.

Virginia was in the first pew with a rotten apple. She was going to eat it. Conner tried to stop her but noticed she looked different. The abnormal facial structure and outward signs of her retardation were gone.

"I told you," Becca said as tears streamed down both cheeks. "I told you to have faith."

"Hallelujah," Connor said, realizing that the lump in his jaw was gone. "Praise God."

Mother Mary

The service station looked like the sort of place that a disease might frequent if it had a driver's license and free will. Yet, given the scarcity of pit stops along the way, Liz decided to pull over anyway, thinking that it might be quite a while before she found another place like this out here in the middle of the scrub-infested desert.

"Mother Mary's," the clapboard sign above the entrance to the dingy convenience store read. "The only place this side of Thornmire County for gas." Liz laughed to herself, thinking about the infamous Last Chance Saloon she had seen on so many of the old westerns. As far as she could tell, this was the modern-day equivalent.

Although Liz was hesitant to touch the gas pump for fear of contracting some exotic germ that might cause her hand to rot off at the wrist, she had no other choice given that all fueling bays were marked self-service. Hesitantly, she used the tail of her shirt to grab the pump and inserted it into the tank. As she did, a spider scurried up the hose. Another one soon followed behind it, leaving a thin wisp of silk behind. If the webs left by the fleeing arachnids were any indication, the pumps hadn't been used in quite a while. Undeterred, Liz squeezed down on the handle and waited for the attendant inside to hit the button that would send a dozen gallons of gasoline into her fuel tank. But nothing happened. Then Liz noticed the 'Please pay first' sign which had been taped just below the octane rating. Sighing at the inconvenience yet thankful that she had been given a reprieve from touching the slimy gas pump, Liz headed inside, wondering why they couldn't have had one of those credit card machines installed out on the island.

As it turned out, Mother Mary wasn't minding the counter. Instead, there was a wrinkled-up prune of a man whose name had been ceremoniously sewn onto his shirt standing next to the cash register, grinning to show the shreds of tobacco that had gotten stuck between his teeth. Bentley, the shirt read. With a cheek full of Red Man and a few teeth missing from his mouth, the ill-named Bentley was about as far from a Rolls Royce as you could get. A 1950s Ford pickup was more like it.

"How'd do, ma'am?" Bentley said with a tobacco-flecked grin. "Need gas, I would imagine?"

Liz nodded, her eyes wandering from Bentley to the huge neon sign that read "Mother Mary's" and back again to the unsightly clerk. "Is there really a Mother Mary, or is that just a cutesy name somebody thought up to pull in lonely truckers?"

"Oh, there's definitely a Mother Mary, and there ain't many rig operators that would drive up mistaking her for a mistress. You can bet your bottom dollar she's around here somewhere, though," Bentley said as he took the ten-dollar bill from Liz, touching her hand for just a bit longer than was necessary to grab the money. "You may see her before you leave. She has a certain fondness for customers."

Although he was crude in a backwoods sort of way, there was something about Bentley that reminded Liz of her father, notwithstanding the bits of tobacco that marked his smile like blacked-out teeth. Maybe it was the way he combed his hair. Or maybe it was that sparkle in his eye that held her fast. Whatever it was, Liz felt simultaneously comforted and slightly alarmed by the man. While she was vaguely reminded of her dad, Liz knew that her father would have never held onto her hand as long as Bentley did. That was what made her uneasy. But then she stopped to consider that Bentley was an old timer and chalked it up to his slow reflexes. Or loneliness, perhaps. She didn't suppose many people dropped in to talk to Bentley out here in the middle of nowhere.

"You out here all by yourself, ma'am?" he asked politely, pulling at his collar to let a little air in. Liz thought of lying and then decided against it.

"Yeah, it's just me," she said as Bentley adjusted his shirt, noticing the white, puffy scars that ran down either side of the old man's chest. When he noticed that Liz was looking, Bentley quickly pulled the lapels of his work shirt to cover the blemishes.

"Heart attack?" she asked politely, thinking Bentley might have had bypass surgery. "My dad had scars similar to those."

"Something like that," Bentley said, apparently unwilling to talk much about it. "It's not me you should be worried about, though. A pretty young lady needn't be out by herself in the middle of nowhere like you are. Lots of things could happen."

Before Liz had a chance to respond, a spider crawled out from underneath the cash register, stopping in the center of the counter, unsure of where to go. Instinctively, Liz grabbed a rolled-up newspaper from a nearby magazine rack.

"Don't do that," Bentley was quick to say, holding up both hands in a 'stop' gesture.

"I hate spiders," Liz insisted.

"They're not the most pleasant things to have around," Bentley explained. "But they keep the gnats away. And that's quite a feat during the summer months when it gets really hot."

Liz thought to herself that Bentley might have some success keeping the gnats at bay with a bar of soap and a stick of deodorant. Unaware or unconcerned about his lack of hygiene, Bentley quickly scooped the spider up in his cupped hands like a father lifting his newborn son out of the crib. He lowered the spider to the floor and watched it scurry away.

"Is it okay to go ahead and get my gas now?" Liz asked a little more impatiently than she meant to. Like a monkey at a typewriter, Bentley ham-fistedly hit the buttons on the old manual cash register, feigning surprise when the bells and whistles began to go off.

"You've done it now, miss," he said, tugging on the bill of his Peterbilt cap. "For being our twenty-fifth customer of the day, you've just won a free car wash. And I must say it couldn't have happened to a prettier lady than you."

Liz looked at Bentley as if he had just told her she was pregnant with his child. Try as she might, Liz just couldn't imagine twenty-four other people stopping here today for any reason, last resort or not. Still, Bentley was grinning good-naturedly from ear to ear, bits of black tobacco clinging to his teeth and gums like plankton on a ship's hull.

"All I want is some gas," Liz protested, having failed to see any sign of a car wash outside.

"Ma'am, it's free," Bentley was quick to add. "You should take advantage of the offer because you won't be able to get one anywhere else for quite a while. Every other town nearby is under a water ban. They won't allow what little water they have to be wasted on dusty cars and trucks."

Liz thought it odd that all neighboring counties had a restricted use of water while Mother Mary's was giving away free car washes. Then again, the offer might have simply been Bentley's way of trying to pick her up, an old man flirting with a younger woman that he couldn't possibly catch with his snaggle-toothed grin, balding head, and prune face. She was reminded of that brief moment when he touched her hand just a second longer than was normal. In ordinary circumstances, Liz might have felt flattered, but out here in the scorching desert, she felt a little apprehensive. Nobody knew that she had gone out of town. Therefore, nobody would even know where to start looking for her if anything went wrong. Liz made a mental note to call somebody as soon as she got her gas and found somewhere a little more suitable up the road to stop.

"I'd really rather get my gas and go if you don't mind," she said as gently as she could, flashing Bentley a smile, hoping it would do the trick.

"I do mind," the old codger said more forcefully than before. "Mother Mary won't be happy if I don't treat the customer right."

"Fine," Liz sighed, "I'll take the car wash. Now, can I go and get my gas?"

"The wash comes first," Bentley insisted.

"Whatever," Liz conceded, thinking it odd how much emphasis Bentley was placing on her free car wash. Surely, Mother Mary wouldn't hold him accountable if she declined the offer. Yet, it didn't seem like Bentley was going to take no for an answer, whatever the consequences. It certainly seemed odd, and while Bentley didn't really seem like much of a threat, Liz wasn't about to take any chances.

She tried to convince herself that Bentley was just a harmless old coot. Still, she knew that a lot of women had gotten themselves killed because of naivete. Trying hard not to show her apprehension, Liz began to think of everything in her purse that she might be able to use if things got out of hand and Bentley didn't turn on the gas pump like he'd promised. Frustrated and beginning to sweat just a little, all Liz could remember was tampons, lipstick, loose change, moist towelettes, chewing gum, nothing that might give her an advantage if things turned nasty. Of course, she always had the whistle that she carried while walking through the park at night. But out here, there wouldn't be anyone to hear it. Which meant that she was in deep trouble if Bentley was lying about the car wash.

"When your car is finished, I'll turn on the pump," Bentley said with a smile. "Just humor an old man, would ya? It makes my job so much easier."

"It appears that I don't have much choice," Liz said with a sigh.

Certainly, Liz could have gotten in her car and driven away at this point, but she wasn't at all sure how far it was to another gas station. The Accord still had about an eighth of a tank of fuel, but judging from the sparsity of rest stops along the way, it was probably another half hour before she saw any sign of civilization. An eighth of a tank certainly wouldn't get her that far.

"Where do I pull my car?" she finally said, reluctant to go along with this but having no other choice.

"I thought you'd see it my way," Bentley said, flashing his black teeth. "Just pull around to the back of the building. You'll see the car wash. It's a drive-through. All you have to do is stay inside and keep your windows rolled up. We'll take care of everything else."

"Fine," Liz said curtly and walked out.

Immediately, the heat slapped her in the face like an abusive boyfriend, and it became hard to breathe. During the few minutes she had stood there at the counter arguing with Bentley, the brisk wind had covered her Accord in a fine layer of beige desert dust. Putting a hand over her nose and mouth to keep from sucking in the harsh sand, Liz quickly removed the gas nozzle from her tank, threw the car door open, and got inside, shutting herself in before the dirt could follow. Then she pulled around to the car wash and hit the brakes.

Like Bentley, everything inside the drive-through looked like it had been out in the sun, baking and withering and drying up, covered with dust from top to bottom as if the water hadn't been turned on in years. It was dark inside the car wash, and Liz hesitantly turned on her lights, her hand on the gearshift, ready to put the Accord in reverse if need be. The bodies of several dead animals littered the floor of the small building like shriveled tumbleweeds that might blow away at any minute. Liz could pick out what looked like a couple of rabbits, a dog, and a coyote. The rest was a mishmash of roadkill that somebody had presumably dragged into the shade to keep the stench at bay.

Cobwebs clung to the cleaning mechanisms of the car wash like a second skin, and Liz could only imagine what sorts of creepy crawlies might come out of the woodworks if the water ever did penetrate their dark, unused hovel. Out of curiosity more than anything else, Liz eased the car forward, letting the headlights penetrate the darkness. In her rearview mirror, she could still see the desert, shimmering like a gong that had been hit several times with a well-placed mallet. It was a reassuring sight. What wasn't reassuring, however, was watching Bentley drag the heavy warehouse door across its track behind her, blocking out sunlight, sand, and the open road, leaving her in complete and total darkness with only the bodies of several decaying animals for company.

"Hey," she screamed. "What are you doing?" But there was no way Bentley could have possibly heard her. Or maybe he would have ignored her anyway.

Not wanting to smell the stench of hot, rotten roadkill, Liz kept her windows up and turned the air conditioning off. Until now, the thought hadn't really crossed her mind that Bentley might be seriously dangerous. Yes, he was crude and made her desperately want to go and take a shower to violently scrub those places where his eyes had wandered over her exposed skin, but he also looked as old and harmless as the dirt that was swirling around outside in lazy whirlwinds. Of course, he had managed to lock her inside of an old car wash that obviously hadn't been used in years. Which meant that even at his age, he still had a few tricks up his dusty unwashed sleeve.

Liz began to grow impatient at the waiting and sat down on the horn, knowing all the while that it probably wouldn't do any good. Not surprisingly, Bentley didn't respond, but one of the dead animals did. The dog that was more skeleton than flesh raised its head and turned to look directly into the headlights at Liz, its eyes shining dully like unpolished marbles. Liz immediately let off the horn, and the dog collapsed to the floor.

Apparently, she'd been wrong about the mutt. It wasn't quite as dead as she had first thought. It was moving, and dead animals didn't simply decide to come back to life. Obviously, it was very, very sick. But not dead. Certainly not dead. The horn must have hurt its ears. Liz tested that theory and laid down on the horn again. This time the coyote rose up with the dog, its mouth open as though it might howl at the moon at any moment. Liz stopped honking. Both animals fell to the dusty floor, their ribs showing through the thin windows of flesh like prison bars.

Now Liz had plenty of reasons to be frightened besides Bentley. The coyote's head lolled at an unnatural angle that was undoubtedly the result of a broken neck, and yet, at the sound of the Accord's horn, it rose up again like a zombie from graveyard dirt. The coyote was dead, and Liz suspected that the dog was in a similar shape.

From this distance, it was impossible to tell anything about the two mangled animals, yet Liz could see enough to discern that something was moving along the dead skin, inside the open mouths, in every gaping wound. Maggots, presumably. It made Liz sick just to think about it. It also made her wonder what sort of microbes were floating around inside the car wash and what sort of things she might have inhaled via the car's ventilation system before she turned off the air conditioning. Something had obviously killed those animals. And yet the dog and coyote were animated to a degree. Undoubtedly, Bentley knew what was out here and was probably enjoying himself immensely at her expense. That's why Liz was determined not to panic. She was at Bentley's mercy until he decided to let her go, and she knew that the only way she would ever get out of the musty car wash would be to cooperate with him. Cautiously, Liz covered her mouth and nose with the tail of her shirt and stepped out of the Accord so that Bentley would be able to hear her when she spoke.

"Okay, Bentley, I'll do whatever you want. Just open the door and let me out."

She heard Bentley laughing, and understandably, it frightened her just a little.

"I think you've got this all wrong," Bentley cackled. "This ain't about what Bentley wants. Bentley's name ain't the one on the sign outside. The best I can remember, that sign says Mother Mary's. She's the one you're here for."

With so much else transpiring around her, Liz had forgotten all about Mother Mary. Naively, she had assumed that Mother Mary was a nice little old lady who hobbled about the store with her walking cane and tobacco pipe planted firmly between her lips. Now, she knew that her impression of things had been wrong.

The lights of the Accord weren't nearly bright enough to light up the entire car wash, yet there was enough illumination to show Liz that something was moving up in the rafters, scurrying among the heavy rotors that turned the massive water brushes. Suddenly very scared, Liz tried to get back into the car but found that her foot was stuck fast to the floor and to the thick patch of web beneath her.

Tugging with all her might, she found that her feet weren't going to budge as long as they were firmly implanted in the sneaker. Quickly, she untied her shoes and stepped out of them, jumping into the car, making sure not to touch the ground again. Hoping to get a better view of what was going on around her, Liz hit her high beams and watched as the gruesome scene in front of her came to life. Tiny spiders, not maggots, hustled over and into the dead carcasses of the slaughtered animals, taking what nourishment they needed and leaving the rest for their brothers and sisters. Thin lines of silk held the animals fast by the head and limbs like marionette strings. Liz pressed down on the horn and watched as all the animals jumped in a bizarre facsimile of life. The rabbits bounced up and down where they had fallen. The dog's mouth fell open, its tongue rolling out like a red carpet. The coyote's head bounced from side to side like a dash ornament mounted on a spring. Suddenly, Liz knew what sort of puppeteer had been maneuvering the animals to the siren's call of her horn.

Mother Mary.

The longer Liz blared the Accord's wimpy horn, the more the animals danced. Then, without warning, a scream pierced through the cacophony, sounding like it came from above her. Keeping one hand pressed down hard on the steering wheel, understanding that the noise was something that Mother Mary didn't like, Liz used the other to crank the car. If Bentley wasn't going to open the door, then she was just going to make a new one.

But Mother Mary, it seemed, had other ideas. The car roof caved in as though it were made of thin, cheap tin, and Liz had to duck to keep from striking her head. Two large, spiky legs pierced the ceiling, one knocking out the dome light, the other missing Liz by only inches. She screamed, matching Mother Mary decibel for decibel. Not enjoying the horn at all, Mother Mary clambered onto the hood, all red eyes and hairy, black appendages, and rammed one leg like a javelin into the source of the noise. The horn went instantly quiet. The darkness soon followed as the headlights were broken one by one.

It was suddenly very quiet inside the car wash. Slow tears burning their way down her face, Liz listened intently for any sign of movement. All she heard instead was the thudding of her own heart. And the sound of the door being slid back on its track. Liz hoped that Bentley had finally decided to take her up on the offer she'd made earlier. At this point, she would really do anything he wanted, if only to escape. As it was, the door only opened enough to let a narrow beam of sunlight in, striking the coyote dead in the face and sending thousands of baby arachnids scuttling off into the darkness. Liz could see through what was left of her rearview mirror that Bentley was smiling.

"Do you see what I've brought you?" Bentley said, his voice audible through the holes that Mother Mary had made in the roof. "I think you'll like her."

Like the chattering of a thousand souls, Mother Mary warbled her reply. The smile quickly faded from Bentley's face.

"You won't have to worry about that noise anymore," he said defensively.

Liz remembered the panic whistle that she kept in her purse in case anyone ever tried to mug or rape her. Ducking her head so she wouldn't scrape her brow on the protruding jagged metal of the collapsed roof, Liz leaned over and searched until her hand happened upon the leather strap of her handbag. In a matter of seconds, she had the whistle in her mouth and blew with every bit of air she had in her lungs. Mother Mary shrieked, and this time Bentley joined in the chorus, shrieking along with her.

Bentley's chest exploded as the shrill screeching of the whistle undoubtedly disturbed what had been lying dormant inside of him. The scars that had been made so many months ago split open like the seams of a pillow that has been stuffed to the bursting point. A cascade of spiders spilled out everywhere, immediately taking what sustenance they could from the withered, leathery attendant.

Taking this as her cue, Liz slammed the gearshift into reverse and hit the gas hard enough to give her a stone bruise on the ball of her sock-covered foot. The door gave easily, nearly torn out of the track, and the sunlight showed Liz a lot more than she ever wanted to see. Many-eyed and writhing in the sun, Mother Mary was about the size of a Harley Davidson motorcycle and nearly as sleek, jaws working like well-oiled vices to tear apart what was left of

Bentley, the man who had unwittingly carried her children inside of him like a surrogate mother.

Not wanting to see any more of the grim spectacle, Liz turned the car around and swerved out of the dusty parking lot in a cloud of dust and a spray of gravel. Although she knew speeding would drain her already-depleted reserves of gas, Liz floored the accelerator and didn't let up until she had left Mother Mary far on the other side of the quicksilver mirage that shimmered in her side mirrors. It was only after she had gotten several miles down the road that Liz noticed the fuel needle and saw the orange light that had flashed on to tell her it was time to fill up her tank. But there was nothing for miles but desert and scrub and shimmering waves of heat coming off the blacktop. There was also the tiny spider that scurried across the cracked dashboard of her car. This time without Bentley there to keep her from it, Liz smashed the spider with the palm of her hand, enjoying the way its death felt against her skin.

One down, she thought grimly, and at least a million more to go.

Intermission II

Max couldn't accept that what he was seeing was real. Not anymore. The last two visions he had glimpsed using Magnusson's Eye stretched his believability to its breaking point. He thought of the giant spider named Mother Mary and mused that it wasn't unlike the plethora of enormous killer bug movies made in the '50s that were social commentaries on the dangers of nuclear testing. But no movie studio had made the films he had watched.

The longer he stayed inside the museum, the more he was tempting fate. Max knew that he should be long gone by now, with the glass eye safely tucked away in his pocket. Exploring the museum only increased the chance of getting caught by the police. He was certain that he had disabled all of the security sensors, the surveillance cameras, and all the alarms. Still, that warning he had seen earlier made him uneasy for reasons he couldn't quite explain: "Beware! Our items are protected!"

Were there security features in the museum that he had overlooked? Cameras he had missed? Silent alarms he had neglected and accidentally tripped? Maybe the police were on their way now. Maybe he would leave the museum and find a bunch of service revolvers pointed at his chest. He didn't think that was the case, but he couldn't be sure.

Beware! Our items are protected!

"Maybe they were protected at one point," Max muttered to himself. "But that was before I arrived on the scene."

Instead of going with his head which told him in no uncertain terms to get out while he could, Max decided to go with his gut and investigate a bit more. Things had changed in the span of the last half hour. That the glass eye was special and potentially valuable, Max had no doubt. But he needed to know more before he simply turned it over to a stranger with a peculiar name who was willing to spend an absurd amount of money on something that looked like it had been picked up at a yard sale.

His lockpicks made short work of the office lock, and he had no trouble gaining access to an antiquated filing cabinet that had seen better days. He was thankful that the museum hadn't successfully made the shift from paper to digital files and was still stuck in the '50s, right along with all the enormous radiation-grown bug movies of the sci-fi era. It made finding a folder with information about Magnusson's Eye fairly easy and quick.

Most of the information about the eye was the same information he had already read on the display. Yet, there was a letter from Marcus Magnusson himself tucked away in the file that provided a considerable amount of illumination on things... or clouded the matter completely depending on how you looked at it and whether or not you believed what the letter said.

"I'm writing this account of what I've discovered in case something happens to me. The eye can be used to find anything hidden, not just monsters. I'm thinking I could use it to find buried treasure. The only catch is that I would need a piece of the original treasure. The eye works almost the same way as a bloodhound works. It needs something to lock on to."

Max's heart pounded in his chest. Suddenly, lots of things made sense, making it fully apparent why The Antiquarian wanted the eye. Fifty grand was a small investment to make in order to net millions in return.

Max returned the file to its rightful place in the cabinet and raced back to the Hall of Monsters. He needed to see more. More likely than not, The Antiquarian didn't think Max would care much about the old piece of junk or suspect that it might be the key to finding millions of dollars in hidden wealth.

Max chose another creature trophy from the shadow box, gripped Magnusson's Eye tightly, and closed his eyes to glimpse the story behind the relic, never noticing the sinister gathering of shadows that were pooling at the end of the hallway.

The Trophy

The hunter surveyed the mantle over the fireplace, studying the trophies he had collected over the years. There wasn't much out there he hadn't killed at one point or another, and the arrangement of animal heads was a testament to his skill in the woods. A twelve-point buck with an impressive three-foot spread was the centerpiece, flanked on either side by a mangy bobcat with curved fangs and a silver-haired coyote that looked like it could have made a warm winter coat. A razorback with nasty-looking tusks was situated on the far left, while the right was taken up by the head of an alligator with a cavernous mouth filled with wicked teeth. The hunter had definitely been busy as of late, and the variety of skulls on public display were a testament to that. Yet, there was still one trophy that eluded him, one more that was needed to make his collection complete: the Woodswalker. However, much to his dismay, hunting season was nearly over. He only had another day or two—maybe not even that long—to bag his prey. If he didn't catch his quarry soon, it would be next season before he had a chance to try again. Of course, by then, he would have to start all over, and that simply wasn't acceptable.

Museum Nocturnus

To make matters worse, one of the Woodswalkers had been inside his cabin recently, judging by the heavy concentration of the stink. He could smell where the creature had been and was able to tell what rooms it had explored and which ones it had steered clear of simply by taking deep breaths. The smell was like a roadmap, and the hunter was loath to follow it. The creature's horrid scent was cloying, covering everything like the spray of a skunk.

Then, there were the footprints to confirm that a prowler had been inside. They were muddy and showed a distinct set of toes, the ball of a foot, and a definite heel. The hunter marveled at just how similar it was to his own foot. He didn't understand how something so similar could be so completely and totally alien to him.

If the invasion of his domain wasn't reason enough to hunt the beast down and kill it, then he didn't know what was. Of course, this technically wasn't his cabin. Still, he had come to think of it as such over the past couple of years, and nothing had challenged his authority here. So, he had stayed, thinking this was easier than living out in the wild.

The hunter had always spent his summers outdoors, sleeping under the stars, just the way God intended. But one day, he stumbled upon the old, rundown shack, found it habitable enough, and decided to stay until someone made him leave. So far, no one ever had, and he had come to think of it as his own. Today, however, one of the Woodswalkers had found him in his own domain and tainted the place with its stink. That meant he wasn't safe, leaving only one of two options. He would hunt it and kill it, or it would do the same to him.

He didn't plan to die today.

He remembered his mother warning him and his siblings about the dangerous Woodswalkers. He had spent many sleepless nights in his youth dreaming of what one might look like up close, how ferocious it might be, what it might do to him if it caught him. Some of that fear slowly crept back in, and the hunter involuntarily shivered, still studying the muddy footprints that tracked across the wooden floor.

He had spotted a Woodswalker once two summers before passing through the forest, and he had been looking for another ever since. That day had given him only a glimpse of what the thing looked like, yet he knew what it was immediately. He had never forgotten what he saw that day, and ever since, it had been a sort of personal mission to track one down again. That was what it would take to complete his collection. That was the trophy that would put all others to shame.

The smell was strong enough that he decided to follow it and see where it led. With any luck, today might be the day he completed his collection. In most respects, the day was just a normal summer day. The sun seemed intent on baking everything in miserable, gasp-inducing heat. Everything was still in the forest, and there were no breezes passing through to cool things off. Even the lake water was too warm to be of much comfort.

Museum Nocturnus

The woods were well-lit. Birds sang high in the boughs of so many pine trees. The forest floor was carpeted with a thick layer of sticky needles. Before coming back to find that his home had been invaded, the hunter had spent most of the day tracking a black bear that would make a nice addition to the cabin when the trail went cold. Now, following the creature's stink, he went in the opposite direction of the bear, heading down to the lake. He could find bears any old day of the week. Today's prize was something much different, much more dangerous.

The lake water was tepid and not really all that comforting. The hunter waded in far enough that he could turn around and survey the land in every direction. The hunter scanned the horizon quickly, searching for any sign of the cabin's intruder.

He was just about to give up and start searching another part of the woods when he heard a strange sound coming from the forest. He whirled in the direction of the noise and was surprised to see a Woodswalker standing upright on two legs staring back at him.

In some respects, the creature was built a lot like he was. In others, it was completely different. Of course, he had heard the stories about these walkers of the woods, and seeing one in the flesh for the second time in his life made all of the stories instantly become real. The creature was covered in thick, coarse hair from head to toe. It stared at him with eyes that were like arrowheads, sharp and piercing. Its feet were hairy and made tracks wherever it walked. It strode across the clearing, staring at him, swinging its arms, daring the hunter to make a move.

The hunter froze, unsure of whether he was up to the challenge. He had killed most everything Mother Nature had been able to throw at him, and this should have been no different. Yet, the Woodswalker was too similar to him in so many ways. It walked like he walked. It hunted as he hunted. The creature seemed to think it held supremacy in these woods. It was almost like killing a distorted mirror image of himself. It was almost like murder.

The creature made a sound that was part scream and part exclamation before fleeing back into the timber line, and the hunter realized in that moment, upon hearing that wild, raucous call, that they were nothing at all alike. The hunter again remembered his mother cautioning him about these villains when he was very young and debated whether or not to pursue it. He thought of the empty space among his trophies that would be perfect for the head of one such as this and disregarded all dangers. Wading out of the water as quickly as he could, he gave chase, unwilling to let the thing get away. This was his chance to catch something he had never caught before.

The chase took him through the underbrush, through thickets filled with thorns and briars, through patches of forest so dense he had to force his way through without regard to what damage he might be doing to his own body. A couple of times, he was certain the Woodswalker had gotten away, then he managed to catch a whiff of its scent on the wind. The things smelled horrible, and it wasn't difficult to follow the stench. That part of the story was true, too. He wondered how many other things about the story would be proven once he caught up to it. Would it be violent? Would it be murderous?

Surely, this Woodswalker must be a killer like all the others. It had to be. His mother had told him about the time a Woodswalker had entered the woods under the cover of dark and abducted one of his cousins. The only remaining evidence of that cousin was a trail of blood, and everyone knew what that meant. His cousin had never been seen or heard from again. Of course, he didn't know the cousin, and none of his other relatives admitted to ever knowing the cousin either. Still, he didn't question his mother's stern warning. She had managed to keep him and his brothers alive all these years, and he had no reason to doubt her now.

The hunter was fast on his feet and ran with reckless abandon. At first, the Woodswalker was just a speck moving ahead of him, leaping over fallen trees, weaving in and out of thickets, and madly flailing his arms, pushing through all of the new growth that impeded his path. Yet, the longer they ran, the closer he got to his prey. He could see the Woodswalker's hair flowing in the wind behind him, and he imagined what that pelt might look like as a rug on the floor of his hovel. He ran faster, ever faster, his goal nearly within reach now.

The Woodswalker, however, was nothing if not full of surprises. The hunter had just about caught his prey when the Woodswalker turned and rushed in his direction with a shout. The hunter wasn't fast enough to avoid what felt like a claw swipe through his midriff, drawing blood and pain in equal amounts. He roared and clutched his abdomen, feeling the warm currents of his life leaking through his fingers. The cut wasn't very deep, but it proved his adversary was as dangerous as his mother had said.

The hunter took a hard swipe at the Woodswalker and connected with the creature's face. The Woodswalker shouted and lunged at him again, this time catching him in the thigh with his claw. Blood spurted in a violent, crimson arc, and the hunter roared. His rage only fueled his attack, and this time he hit the Woodswalker with all he had, slamming the creature into a nearby tree. The Woodswalker groaned and fell to the ground, unable to fight anymore. The hunter was injured but couldn't take time to consider his own wounds. He needed to move quickly so he could get the Woodswalker back to the cabin... and to the rest of the trophies.

He bled all the way back home, but he ignored the burning in his stomach and leg. He had to. This was the time to show his superiority over the Woodswalker and to exact his revenge for the way the foul-smelling creature had invaded his sanctuary.

He was afraid the Woodswalker would wake up and stage a revolt on the way back, but the creature had sustained a nasty head wound during the attack. The creature didn't move or stir. Satisfied he had time to tend to his own wounds, the hunter headed back down to the lake.

He knelt on the shore, scooping up handfuls of mud and packing them against the cuts he had sustained, stanching the flow of blood. Gradually, the mud crusted into a paste of sorts, eventually drying out and sealing the wounds. It wasn't a perfect treatment for such nasty cuts, but it would have to do. At least the bleeding had stopped. That was the main thing.

The hunter hobbled back to the cabin, thinking about what he was going to do. It was one thing to kill a creature in the heat of the moment. It was another thing to slaughter something that was unconscious and not putting up a fight. When he walked back in, the Woodswalker was just as he had left him, lying on the floor, chest gently moving up and down with each shallow breath.

The creature's face had softened in sleep, and he didn't look nearly as menacing now as he once had. The hunter only had to twist the wrong way and awaken the pain in his midriff to remember this wasn't some harmless herbivore. This Woodswalker was every bit the hunter he was, and equally as vicious.

He needed to make his move now before the Woodswalker woke up and tried to defend himself. Summoning up his courage, he approached his prey, intent on ripping its head off and adding it to the others sitting atop the fireplace. Then, he noticed something that gave him pause.

The creature looked hirsute from a distance, yet up close, it seemed the hair wasn't real. The thick brown skin and tangled knots of pelt lay over the Woodswalker like a second skin, one that wasn't attached. The hunter knelt down and pulled at it. The creature's arm pulled out of the skin easily, and the other arm pulled out as well. He soon found himself holding a hide of some sort that was covered in dark, matted hair. He looked at the feet, all dense walnut fringe and thick, leathery soles. He pulled at one of them, and it slid off easily, revealing a foot that was much different from the hunter's own. The Woodswalker's foot was light-skinned and much smaller than his. It was smooth and not hairy at all.

The hunter wasn't quite sure what to make of all this. He was confused. Yet, what confused him more than anything else was when the Woodswalker opened his eyes slowly, looked over at him, and spoke. "Please, don't kill me," it said. "You can have my cabin. You can have whatever you want. Just don't hurt me."

The hunter knelt down beside the Woodswalker and lifted one of the creature's hands, searching for the lethal claws that had nearly disemboweled him earlier. Its hands were free of any sort of chitinous weapon. This was not at all the sort of devil he had imagined he was chasing. This was not the creature his mother had told them about.

So, what was he supposed to do? Just kill it and forget about everything he had learned so far? Let it go?

He didn't know what to do at this point. All he knew was that he was weak from so much blood loss. Whatever he was going to do, he needed to do it quickly.

He stood and took a step toward the Woodswalker and felt the strength leave his legs. He nearly collapsed but somehow managed to remain on his feet. The mud he'd packed on his wounds had stopped working, and the wounds were bleeding freely again. The hunter roared in frustration and stomped his overly large feet on the pine floor.

The Woodswalker eyed him carefully and pulled something out of its second skin. It was sharp and deadly and quite likely responsible for the pain he was feeling right now. The Woodswalker held it in his hand and staggered to his feet, ignoring the blood that was trickling down its own head. It waved the metal claw confidently in its hand, and the hunter knew that sustaining one more wound might prove fatal.

Yet, the Woodswalker was overconfident, believing he had the upper hand. He charged at the hunter with the claw, and the hunter summoned one last burst of strength, charging at his assailant, knocking the metal claw from his hand. Knowing now he couldn't afford to give this creature any more chances, the hunter did as his mother had taught him and his other hairy, lumbering brothers to do so many years ago. He held the Woodswalker over his head and ripped the head off its body in a mighty display of strength. Although the hunter's wounds were bleeding more freely now, puddling on the floor, and the pain was excruciating, he reveled in his victory, ignoring the hurt for as long as he could before dropping the lifeless body to the ground and trudging over to the mantle with a head in his hand.

Soon, the shelf over the fireplace was overcrowded as one more trophy was added. The Woodswalker's skull stared back at him with dull, glassy eyes.

Grateful this ordeal was over and he had finally claimed his last prize of the season, the hunter lumbered out of the cabin in search of help. He grunted and groaned to get someone's attention, and soon his brethren came out of the woods to lend a hand. They made large footprints in the mud and took gigantic strides toward him, their arms dangling awkwardly at their sides.

Never in all his days had he been so glad to see so many of his own kind forsaking their homes in the woods to come and help him. Yet, he was most grateful to see his mother lumbering out of the underbrush, her once-lustrous brown hair now a regal silver as the years had taken their toll on her. She strode over to him, swinging her arms, moving slowly yet with grand purpose.

The hunter grunted a greeting and made a series of guttural noises that were indecipherable to anyone but his own kind. In his own way, he apologized to his mother for ever doubting her story about the Woodswalker. In an act of forgiveness universal to all mothers, she grunted her reply and began to tend to his wounds.

The hunter let his mother and the others administer to him and drifted off into slumber as the loss of so much blood took its toll on him. Somewhere in the distance came the sound of sirens. The Woodswalkers would be searching for their own soon. Yet, for now, he didn't want to think about that.

Museum Nocturnus

Instead, he thought about trophies and what he might add next to his ever-growing collection.

"My collection is finally complete," the hunter thought to himself as he lost his grip on consciousness. "I got one today. I finally got a human."

Quartet

Part I: Trapped

The conservatory had been built near the ocean, overlooking a white beach that could have been featured on a New England postcard. At times, the roar of the waves and the rush of forceful breezes were all you could hear. Other times it was the frenzied sound of dozens of students running through musical scales and refining their technique by practicing various pieces from the classical masters. The air carried with it a faint stench of brine and fish, but the primary smell that overpowered the senses came from the aromatic groves of sandalwood that grew near the beach. The original founders of The Hayden School of Music hoped that the serenity of the landscape would be a breeding ground for creative genius. Yet, unbeknownst to them, other darker things grew there too.

The children of the sea slumbered in aquatic cocoons beneath the waves. Centuries ago, they had been bound there through a ritual by the early settlers of Valley Falls, who knew the danger they posed. The secret to this binding had been written down in a code of musical notes, disguised as a particularly challenging concerto for a string quartet. The music was untitled yet penned in painstaking detail and hidden away in the archives of the music school. In a world filled with the works of masters like Chopin, Beethoven, Mozart, and Tchaikovsky, no one gave more than a passing glance to an old untitled piece of music written by an unknown composer named Archibald. And so, the composition went unplayed, and the creatures remained trapped.

The children of the sea dreamed restless, bloody dreams and longed for the day that they could be freed from their underwater prisons to come ashore and indulge their perverse appetites. Above all else, they were hungry. So hungry. If only they could find their way to the surface where juicy morsels of flesh were in plentiful supply. But there was something else besides hunger. On a deep, agonizing physiological level, the children of the sea wanted to come ashore and stop the music from the conservatory because of the pain it caused them. The early settlers had discovered the sea creatures' weakness early on and used it to weave a spell that would not only wound and weaken them but bind them to the ocean floor as well. And so, the snippets of music that filtered down to them from the conservatory seemed to mock their predicament and remind them of the arcane performance that had trapped them so far down beneath the surface, leaving them to long for the day that they might be free.

As it turned out, that day was today.

It was the day Gordon decided to move forward with the monumental lie he had told his friends.

Part II: Escape

The members of the string quartet had set up in the practice hall and were busy tuning their instruments. Gordon, a burly bear of a man, ran a hand through his dark beard and picked up his cello. The others grabbed their instruments too and looked to the big man for direction since he was the one who had called this meeting.

"Has everybody practiced their parts?" he asked.

"Aye, aye, captain," Caitlin said as she played with her lip ring.

"Yep," Michelle replied as she exhaled a large cloud of bluish smoke from her lungs. She took another hit of her vape and stuck the device back into her pocket.

"I did," Charlie said as he adjusted his turtleneck.

"Sweet," Gordon said with a sense of satisfaction. "This is going to be awesome."

"Man, I still can't believe you wrote this," Charlie said in awe. "This is amazing. Who knew you were such a genius?"

"Well, me, of course," Gordon said with a hearty laugh. "I've just been waiting for the rest of you losers to figure it out."

"It's awesome," Charlie said. "Sincerely. I didn't even realize you knew Latin."

Gordon pursed his lips and wrinkled his brow. "What do you mean?"

"At the top," Charlie added. "That little note you wrote."

"Oh, yeah," Gordon said, not wanting to elaborate on something he knew nothing about. "You'd be surprised at all the things I know that I keep to myself."

"I'm impressed," Charlie said. "Sincerely."

Gordon nodded in a gesture of thanks and tried to keep the truth from showing on his face. So what if he had plagiarized some old piece of music from the 1800s? He was fairly sure that no one would recognize it. It had no name on it and was jammed back in one of the old filing cabinets in the basement of the archives. Likely, it had been shifted, moved around, and shuffled from one location to another for years before finally getting tucked away for posterity in an old manila folder. If this didn't get him a staff position here, then nothing would. He was, by far, the oldest member of the group and had little to show for his age. Presenting this concerto as his own was supposed to change all of that. Of course, there was always the slim chance that someone might recognize it. But Gordon was willing to roll the dice. This was his shot, and he was determined to go through with it.

"This piece is tough," Caitlin said, fingering the silver ring in her septum. "I think you threw everything in but the kitchen sink. Octaves. String skipping. And the tritone? I hope we don't summon the devil or something when we play this."

"There are only a few people who I would expect to use the 'diabolus in musica' in their original composition," Michelle said. "Gordon is one of them."

Gordon chuckled. "Hey, if it was good enough for the Catholic Church to outlaw, it's good enough for me to use. Now, if everybody's ready, let's see if we can play through this bad boy."

"Wait," Michelle said. "You can't have a composition with no name. What do you call this piece?"

Gordon thought about it for a moment. "In my mind, it sounds like insanity. So, I think I'll name the concerto 'Bedlam', because it's exactly the sort of music I would expect to hear in a mental institution."

"Fitting," Charlie said, still amazed that Gordon was responsible for the music that sat in front of them. In all the years he had known Gordon, he had never suspected that the burly man might be capable of writing something as complex and nuanced as 'Bedlam'. In truth, he was a little jealous. He was the one everyone expected to be great. Gordon was always so mediocre, and no one expected much from him. That's what made his brilliant composition all the more unexpected.

Gordon knew that once they played the piece under the guise that he was its composer, there was no turning back. He would be committed to the deception... and to the consequences. He mulled over the changes it might bring into his life and never once considered that one of those changes might be to place his very life in jeopardy. Instead, he thought about success, peer recognition, and, of course, money. He was broke, and the idea of getting a faculty position that would pay him enough to live on was enough to chase away any misgivings he might have had.

"Let's do this," Gordon said before counting them off.

Not long after the four of them started to play, Gordon realized he had made a very big mistake. Playthrough of the first few measures was uneventful. Then, something started happening. The air began to shimmer in the way it does on a hot desert highway. Strange, dark shapes danced in front of Gordon's eyes. The music transformed, sounding less like melody and more like a key turning in a lock. Gordon's stomach twisted itself into knots. Something felt wrong about the whole thing, but wrong on a level that was indescribable. The music was dark, sinister, foreboding. It was the soundtrack of the apocalypse as played by the Four Horsemen. It was the kind of music that might accompany the end of the world, and the moment he realized it was a gateway to death and destruction, it was too late to turn back.

The other members of the group seemed to realize that something was wrong too, but they didn't stop playing. No one wanted to be the one that ruined the rehearsal. They looked around at each other with uncertainty. Somewhere deep in the most primeval part of their brains that was composed of instinct and self-preservation, they all felt that something was happening around them. On some unconscious level, each of them sensed something ancient and evil opening one sleepy eye. None of them had any idea why such an image had formed in their minds, but the thought of it terrified and chilled them. It was a feeling of foreboding and dread that was inexplicable, yet they were powerless to stop it.

In the dismal depths, the children of the sea sensed it too and opened their eyes as the musical key fitting the lock that bound them drifted down through the murky currents. Music had imprisoned them, and this concerto, a complete reversal of the ritual, set them free.

When the spell was broken, the ground shook, and the earth was torn apart as if by the hands of a giant. Fissures spread across the sea floor. One by one, the denizens of the deep broke free of the stone tomb that had held them captive for so long and floated to the surface, where they bobbed up and down like fishing corks. It had been so long since they had been allowed to roam freely, and many of them stared up at the sky, their overly large eyes gazing in bewilderment at so many curious and perverse sights.

Then, with haste, they headed toward shore.

As a direct result of the earthquake, many of the musicians inside the conservatory died beneath the weight of fallen ceilings or were swallowed up by gaping chasms in the floor. They were the lucky ones. Others managed to escape the earth's wrath entirely, dodging the debris that crashed down around them. Little did they know, the sea's wrath was much, much worse. Those who fled the conservatory ran straight into the waiting mouths of the sea children who were trudging up the beach. The screaming was over in a matter of seconds, and blessed silence filled the music hall.

Of the multitudes of musicians who had been alive and honing their craft before the earthquake, only Gordon's string quartet survived.

Part III: The Sea's Revenge

The practice hall was in shambles. The walls leaned on each other, too weak to stand on their own. Paintings of the conservatory's founders were strewn about the hall, streaked by the wind and the rain that had accompanied the earthquake. Music stands, twisted and gnarled by the tremors, were overturned. Sheet music littered the floor like brittle leaves on an autumn lawn. The windows were little more than jagged teeth of glass after flying debris had broken most of the panes. Spatters of blood marred everything like abstract art.

A gaping black hole was all that remained of the spot where Professor Grady had once stood. One moment, he was standing just outside the door to the practice hall, listening intently to Gordon's concerto and marveling at its complexities. The next, the ground beneath him swallowed him whole as the earthquake shattered the limestone on which the conservatory was built. A series of caverns ran beneath the music school, but that fact had never held any significance until today. Now, hideous, sharp-toothed creatures of the deep could move under the school uninhibited, emerging at just the right time to pluck an unsuspecting morsel from the surface.

Some of the ocean had filtered in through that fissure in the floor, and what was left of the floor was covered with a thin slick of saltwater and wet pages of musical notation. Planks of hardwood flooring around the lip of the pit had splintered with the tremors. Those that hadn't cracked were warped and buckled as the water continued to seep in. A few droplets of blood rimmed the chasm like that of a sacrifice offered up to an elder god. Professor Grady was the offertory lamb that had perished in the depths of that hole. It was there that the musicians kept their vigil. It was almost as if they expected him to crawl out of there at any minute, slick back his gray hair, and rap his baton impatiently to get their attention. Of course, that was never going to happen ever again. There was no possible way Grady could still be alive. Not after the way he had been flung about like a child's toy and then subsequently ripped apart by all of those tentacles.

Even now, none of them were really sure what had happened or what the thing had been that had killed him. One moment, they were playing Gordon's concerto. The next, an earthquake ripped the building apart, allowing chaos to erupt from beneath them. A denizen had emerged from that hole in the floor like some subterranean god with whiplike flagella that were covered in hundreds of thorn-like barbs and a series of mouths that were filled with rows of razor-sharp teeth. It was like watching Professor Grady being eaten alive by a school of piranha. What the creature hadn't eaten of Professor Grady, it had taken below ground. None of the quartet liked to think about what parts of their mentor might actually be left down there, floating in muck and digestive juices.

The mass of whiplike flagella undulating beneath the floor would have probably sunk its barbs into each of them and dragged them all to a watery grave if Michelle hadn't inadvertently drawn her bow across the strings of her violin as she scrambled to move as far away from the hole in the floor as possible. Tentacles with suckers as big as dinner plates rose up out of the hole, snaking across the floor in hopes of grabbing another tasty morsel. The single note from Michelle's instrument was like a knife wound, giving the beast room for pause. At the first sound of dissonant noise, the monstrosity in the subfloor shrieked in pain and willfully pulled away from her. Michelle, seeing what had just taken place, played another note, and the creature made a horrible screeching cry that sounded like it was being burned alive. It flailed in the air wildly, allowing her to put even more distance between herself and the blue-gray tentacle.

"Everybody play!" she called out to her friends. "It doesn't like the sound."

The others picked up their instruments too, and began playing whatever came to mind. The sea monster responded dramatically, flailing its tentacles this way and that, thrashing about in hopes of stopping the music. But the musicians had all retreated to the extreme edges of the room where the tentacles couldn't reach as easily and played like their lives depended on it.

Gradually, with each new strain of Mozart or Beethoven, the beast could be heard slinking away, splashing through the wet tunnels in the limestone. Each of the musicians held their breath and waited for the monster to return for round two. All of them played diligently in the hopes that their music would keep it at bay.

"It's gone," Charlie said with a sigh, putting his bow down for a moment. Hoping it was safe, the others followed suit. The second they stopped playing was the second they heard screaming. The screaming bore no resemblance to anything that might tear its way out of a human throat. They could hear the wet slither of something navigating the damp limestone tunnels. Nobody needed to see it in person again to know what was responsible for the noise. The screaming crescendoed and sounded closer than before.

"It's coming back!" Charlie screamed as he started playing again. "Everybody play!"

The quartet was fast enough to keep the squid-like monstrosity beneath their feet from rising up through the floor again. But they were a fraction of a second too late where the other monsters were concerned. A phalanx of new deformities had gathered at the broken windows and was feverishly trying to wriggle their bulbous bodies in through openings that were much too small. The earthquake had knocked out most of the power, and shadows were more prevalent than light. But in the meager illumination that remained, the four musicians watched in horror as many of the grotesque amphibian horrors impaled themselves on sharp slivers of glass or spilled their innards while sliding across nasty lingering bits of broken window. None of them actually got in alive, but a handful of the creatures did manage to push themselves all the way through before dying. They flopped spastically on the wet floor before succumbing to their wounds. The others were smart enough not to follow in their dead compatriots' footsteps. Besides, it was clear from their high-pitched squealing that they couldn't stand the music emanating from violin, viola, and cello. They sounded like a throng of angry, drowning pigs-gurgling and screeching all at once.

"What is happening here?" Caitlin asked, her lower lip trembling. "We played Gordon's composition, and the world quickly fell apart around us. The words at the top must have been true."

"What words?" Charlie asked.

"The Latin written at the top of the page," Caitlin said. "Mors ab imis. Didn't anybody else notice them?"

"What do those words mean, Gordon?" Michelle asked.

"I don't know," the big man admitted as he drew his bow across the strings of his instrument.

"How do you not know?" Charlie asked. "You wrote it, didn't you?"

"Of course, I did," Gordon said, unwilling to consider the possibility that the music was responsible for any of the tragedy around them.

"So, what does it mean?" Charlie pressed.

"I don't know what the Latin means," Gordon admitted. "I saw the words on the back of an old horror novel and thought they sounded cool."

"The phrase means 'death from below'," Caitlin explained. "Death certainly came from below. That can't be a coincidence. What is going on?"

No one had an answer to her question. Or at least not an answer that they were willing to share at the moment. It was difficult to play their instruments and carry on a conversation at the same time. For a few moments, no one said anything. Still, Caitlin studied Gordon carefully, her mind working feverishly.

To judge by her pink hair, numerous eyebrow piercings, and black lipstick, abnormality should have been something Caitlin was accustomed to. But her rough punkish exterior hid the scared child that cowered inside. Looks, it seemed, could be deceiving. The bloodthirsty monsters that lived beneath the once-beautiful conservatory were proof enough of that.

Gordon continued to play his cello confidently without missing a single note. He was acutely aware that Caitlin was eyeballing him. She suspected that something was off with that composition. Of course, he hadn't written it. But that didn't mean it was responsible for all the death and destruction around them. That was absurd.

"Get it together, Gordon," he thought to himself.

"All of this is happening because of the earthquake," he said, speaking loudly so his voice could be heard over the music. "Those tremors must have let all of these things out into the world."

"What do you mean?" Michelle asked.

Gordon sighed and played a few lines from Slayer's "Seasons in the Abyss" before explaining himself. "This conservatory is built on top of a series of limestone tunnels. My best guess is that this race of subterranean beasts lives there, sleeping. The earthquake woke those monsters up."

"Is it possible someone else has survived?" Michelle asked. "Someone has to be coming to help us. Right?"

Charlie sighed as he moved one hand up the wet neck of his viola. "The earth's still shifting," he said at last. "One good aftershock could still kill us all. For all our sakes, we better hope there are other survivors."

"So how do we find out for sure?" Caitlin asked, each word showing just a flash of her silver tongue spike. "Those things will rip us to pieces."

"I'm going to count to three," Charlie said. "Everyone stop playing for two seconds and listen. If we hear music, we'll assume that somebody else has managed to stay alive. If not, we'll know that we're the only ones left."

Everyone nodded. "Sounds logical enough," Gordon agreed.

"Okay," Charlie said nervously. "One. Two. Three."

Three brief seconds of complete silence was all it took to destroy what little hope the string quartet had. In that brief vacuum of quiet, there remained only the ghosts of music and musicians. The denizens of the deep had been efficient in their invasion of the conservatory.

The moment the music stopped, a phalanx of tentacles erupted from the hole in the center of the floor, grasping for any sort of purchase in the flooded practice room.

"Play!" Caitlin shrieked even though no one needed to be told. Each of them drew their bows across the sweat-soaked strings, praying that their notes would be enough protection from the gruesome barbed tentacles and the sawblade mouths that awaited the taste of tender flesh. It was all the four of them could do to stay in their seats and not run screaming down the blood-soaked hallways of the conservatory. Of course that would have been suicide.

"I guess we've got our answer," Charlie said grimly as he simultaneously tried to play and wipe the sweat off his brow with one of his shirtsleeves. "The four of us are all that remain. And those beasts are just waiting to tear us apart. All they need is a window of silence, and we're dead."

"Am I the only one who finds it odd that Gordon suddenly becomes brilliant enough to write a concerto that just happens to have a note at the top that translates into 'death from below' in Latin, then, as we're playing, death does, in fact, come from below in the form of a bunch of barnacle-covered fish-men and some tentacled monstrosity beneath the floor that might rise up at any moment and devour us whole?"

"What are you trying to say?" Gordon said. "That I caused all of this?"

Caitlin leveled her gaze at him. "Maybe not on purpose. But be honest with us. Did you write that piece of music?"

Part IV: Aftershock

Gordon was just about to respond to Caitlin's accusation when an aftershock ripped its way up through the rock like a demon child tearing its way out of a womb. Every member of the quartet was thrown from their chairs, leaving the practice hall devoid of all music save for the melodies of chaos: the cracking of walls, the sharp gunfire report of rock breaking in half, the angry shriek of the faces at the windows as they were thrown to and fro. Although it was a frightening event to live through, it was also somewhat of a comfort to see the fish creatures scrambling about in disarray and terror. The subaquatic god that was waiting just beneath the surface, however, wasn't as susceptible to the tremors of the earth. Without the music there to drive them back, the tentacles rose up out of the trembling pit, slithering and snaking across the floor in search of human purchase. One of the vine-like flagella wrapped itself around Michelle's leg and began pulling her toward the open maw in the floor. Water and pages of musical notation sloshed around her, leaving foam and bits of music in her wake. She screamed for help. Charlie grabbed Michelle's hand and pulled her toward him. She screamed as the tentacle's sharp barbs tore deep gashes in her leg.

Ragged chunks of ceiling plaster broke loose and rained down from above. The floor buckled and swayed, creating small waves inside the practice hall. Meanwhile, new tributaries of ocean filtered in as the limestone beneath the subfloor crumbled away, leaving some parts of the room under six inches of water. Tentacles rushed through the water like an army of snakes.

Gordon kicked angrily at the tentacles that were floating atop the water. Caitlin rammed the leg of one of the metal music stands into the thick mass of bluish flesh. Hurt and angry, the squid-beast roared from the pit and immediately pulled back.

Still a bit unsteady, Gordon and Caitlin got to their feet. It was then that they saw Charlie. He was unconscious. One of the falling chunks of plaster had struck him in the back of the head.

"Get his head up!" Gordon screamed. At first, Michelle didn't realize what he was talking about. Her leg was bleeding copiously, and she had been busy trying to stanch the flow of blood. Then she turned around and saw Charlie slumped over. Blood trickled down the back of his head. His face was submerged beneath the water. An egg-sized knot was forming just over his left ear.

Frantic, Michelle disregarded her wounded leg and yanked Charlie's head up out of the water while Gordon and Caitlin maneuvered him onto his back.

"Charlie, wake up," Michelle said, slapping his cheeks hard enough to rouse him. Charlie groaned and opened his eyes. He rubbed the knot on his head with an unsteady hand.

"Are you okay?" Michelle asked him.

Charlie winced at the pain that ran from the knot all the way down his neck and then nodded. "I'm not great, but I can play."

Gordon and Caitlin rushed back to their instruments. They knew it wouldn't be long now before the denizens returned, maybe with reinforcements freed during the second quake.

Predictably, the bulbous, glassy-eyed faces leered at them as they played, waiting for that one moment of weakness when the instruments crashed to the ground, and the glorious silence allowed them the chance to enter and pillage at will. But the musicians were resolute in their playing. They had to be.

Exhausted from the grueling practice session and the shock of nearly getting killed, all of the musicians were sweating. Even now, the muscles in Charlie's hand were starting to throb. Looking around at his partners, he could see that they were getting a little tired too.

"My hand's cramping up," Gordon said as he drew the bow across the cello's string. The instrument sighed like a discontented child. "We've been at this non-stop for hours. We'll have to rest sometime. Maybe we could play in shifts."

"I don't think that's a very good idea," Charlie said, fretting his viola even though the callouses on the tips of his fingers were starting to soften and grow sore. "The music four of us make is enough to keep the monsters at bay. And it might be just enough. The loss of one, however, might mean the death of us all. It's like taking one brick out of a dam. That's all that's needed for a flood."

"So we just play until we collapse, and then the mermen at the window burst in and eat us alive? Have you noticed the teeth they've got in those mouths?"

"You're being melodramatic," Charlie said. "All I said is that I didn't think it was a good idea. Of course, there's no way we can play indefinitely, so I guess we'll have to chance it and see what happens. Just be ready to start playing again the moment those beasties show any signs of movement. I don't want to die because of your weak hand."

"I don't like it," Caitlin said, taking a glance at one of the broken windows. At the moment, there was no demonic visage waiting there, but that didn't mean there weren't a few of the beasts lurking nearby.

"So, who's going to take the first break?" Michelle shouted at last. "I need to vape. I'm getting twitchy." The wind was starting to gust outside, and the roar of it through the broken windows was nearly as loud as their music. She almost had to scream to be heard.

"Me," Caitlin spoke up before any of the others volunteered. The other three looked at her severely.

"You?" Gordon said indignantly.

"I've got to go to the bathroom," Caitlin cried. "The pain's not extreme yet. But I won't be able to hold it much longer."

"Fine," Gordon said flatly.

"It's okay with me," Michelle agreed.

"Go ahead, Caitlin," Charlie said, finalizing the vote. "We'll cover for you."

Slowly and methodically, Caitlin laid down her violin and stood up. She stretched her arms and bent over to work the kinks out of her back. After so many hours of playing, it was clear that the exercise was much needed. The other three watched her carefully as they played. It was clear that they expected something to grab her at any minute and were relieved when nothing did.

She gave them a placating smile and then crept cautiously toward the door, keeping a safe distance from all the broken windows and the grotesque fin-like appendages that might reach through them. The crevice in the broken floor looked like an ominous mouth that was waiting to swallow her up, and wisely, she steered clear of that as well. Michelle and Charlie, meanwhile, had lapsed into Rachmaninoff. Always the non-conformist, Gordon played something off an old Metallica album. The music wasn't so much music now as it was noise. None of them were playing exactly the same thing, and the result was a cacophony of sound that was reminiscent of the warm-ups that went on in the practice hall before a concert. Still, it did as it was intended to do and kept the monsters at bay.

Caitlin looked around the room for a moment as if searching for something.

"What are you doing?" Michelle yelled at her.

"I want to look at that piece of sheet music," Caitlin said, unwilling to give up on the idea that there was something fishy about Gordon's "Bedlam" concerto.

The color left Gordon's face when he realized that she was trying to find a copy of the sheet music. Granted, they had all had the ability to study the concerto in greater detail before the practice session. But none of them had really scrutinized it for clues that Gordon wasn't the author prior to rehearsal. They hadn't needed to at that point. Things were different now.

"I'll only be a minute," Caitlin assured them. "Just hang on for a little longer."

Unwilling to let this proceed to its logical conclusion, Gordon kept his bow on the strings of his cello but stopped playing. The loss of volume had an immediate effect.

The tentacle that slithered through the door was quick and vicious, like a whip with teeth. Before anyone could make a move to help, the flagella had wrapped itself around Caitlin's throat. Her eyes went wide, and she clutched madly at her throat. But it was no use. The beast was much too strong, tearing her head off as easily as a child would rip the plastic limbs from a baby doll. The body slumped to the floor with a loud thud while Caitlin's head rolled into the massive crevice like a child's ball. Blood spurted in high arcs from the neck like water from a sprinkler head.

"Caitlin!" Gordon shouted, dropping his bow momentarily in a gesture of mock terror.

"Play louder!" Charlie screamed as he saw a slithering flurry of activity beneath the floor. Apparently, the sudden appearance of a human head and the loss of volume from the remaining musicians had stirred the subterranean beast into a frenzy. Peering down into the dark pit, it looked like a nest of snakes had taken up residence. The musicians quivered with the effort of playing so hard and so fast for so long.

"We can't play like this forever," Gordon said, slowing down the pace of his playing for a moment. "We're all going to die once we pass out from exhaustion. This is the end of the world. Or at least our world anyway."

"We have to keep going," Charlie said. "Look over at the windows. Something's obviously working. And we're still alive. That has to count for something, doesn't it?"

Gordon and Michelle both turned their attention toward the fish-men at the windows. Their number had decreased by half.

"Where did the rest of them go?" Michelle asked, her voice taking on a new level of concern.

Somehow, during the fracas, she had found an opportunity to fish out her vape pen. The device jutted from her lips at an odd angle as she spoke each word. It was a symbol of habit, a symbol of ritual. At a time when so much of the familiar was torn apart, it made Michelle feel better to have something of her old routine to hold onto.

"They're on the roof," Gordon said grimly. "They're trying to bring the conservatory down on top of us."

"So that's it then?" Michelle said, tears brimming at the corners of her eyes. "Caitlin's gone for good, and all of us are right behind her. We can't stop playing long enough to do anything, and they know it. They'll do whatever they can to bring the house down on top of us. And all we can do is sit here in this grave and be buried quietly."

Michelle turned to look at her fallen friend one last time and sobbed anew as she discovered that Caitlin's body was gone. The door was ajar. Whatever had removed her head had come back to claim the rest of her. A slick bloody trail led off down the hallway. They had all been too enraptured in playing and discussing the situation to see what was responsible.

"Poor Caitlin," Michelle wept. It was clear from the way her body heaved with sobbing that she was on the verge of dropping her violin. Although it took some effort, Charlie slid his chair toward her. The messy sludge of blood and seawater on the floor made the move a little easier.

"Don't stop now," Charlie said as he drew his own bow across the strings. "One of us had to try our luck."

"Is that why she died?" Michelle asked. "She was looking for a copy of that music. This came just after she accused Gordon of not being the composer. Seems awfully convenient that she died when she did. It sure kept her from pursuing that line of thought."

"Good point," Charlie said. "Anything to say, Gordon?"

"You're both crazy." Gordon scowled. "You can't seriously think I'm responsible for all of this madness."

"Do you have anything to confess?" Charlie asked.

"Only that I hate both of you for thinking such a thing."

"We can't worry about any of that now," Charlie said. "We've got to figure out a way to stay alive."

"I think we should play the Mozart requiem," Michelle said at last, not knowing any other way to show how she felt. "We owe Caitlin that much. She was our friend. We should mourn."

"I agree with that," Gordon said.

"How human of you," Michelle said.

Nobody said anything for a while. It was nice to simply play and ruminate on the memories of the departed. They all had suffered a staggering loss, but they were still alive. And while none of them said it aloud, each of the remaining three hoped that the requiem they were playing wasn't some bleak turn of foreshadowing. Ordinarily, it would have been a harrowing thought. At the moment, however, they were too numb to feel much of anything. Muscles ached. Mouths were dry. Callouses grew sore. Fingers bled. They would have given almost anything to stop for just five minutes, but the price for such a rest break was death.

They played on.

Part V: The Truth

"Okay," Michelle agreed, playing a dissonant note. "Anybody got any good ideas about getting out of here alive?"

"Well," Charlie said, "as a matter of fact, I do. The first thing we should do is to find a radio and try to find some news, see if this sort of thing is breaking out somewhere else."

"Perfect plan," Gordon said sarcastically. "All you need to do is grow yourself a third hand so you can play and dial up a station. We're as good as saved. Honestly, why didn't I think of that?"

"You don't have to be condescending," Charlie snapped as he stood up and began walking slowly around the room in search of a radio.

During his exploration of the room, Charlie made sure to steer clear of the hole in the floor and to continue playing as he walked. Gordon and Michelle watched him with concern. It was clear that they expected something to grab him at any minute and pull him down into one of its myriad mouths. Charlie watched both of them with equal concern. He was genuinely afraid that something might happen to Michelle and fearful that Gordon might stop playing just so the sea god could grab him. He and Gordon had never been on the closest of terms. Those terms were strained even further by their shared affection for Michelle.

Charlie hated to think that Gordon would sink to such levels and murder him in cold blood by simply laying down his bow. Still, it was a possibility he had to consider. Understandably, he wasted no time in his search for a radio.

In addition to the ones on the roof, the remaining creatures were slapping the wet bricks outside. There was also increased movement down in the pit. The denizens were getting impatient. Gordon stuck his tongue out at one of them. He would have done something more obscene, but it would have required the use of hands. Charlie watched him carefully, certain that he was about to be double-crossed. Gordon continued playing for the moment.

Charlie couldn't help noticing that Gordon had scooted his chair closer to Michelle. Thankfully, he had a task to focus on, something to take his mind off his jealousy. He kept trying to tell himself that he was doing this so that he and Michelle might have a chance once this whole thing was over with. It didn't make him feel better when he noticed how Gordon was leering at her.

With some difficulty, Charlie was able to lay his violin down on one of the desks in the room and use one hand to keep drawing the bow across the strings. This left the other hand free to search the drawers for something that would help them escape this hellish landscape. Most of the drawers were filled with sheet music. One of the cabinets had a metronome, baton, and a box of polishing cloths for the brass instruments. The last drawer he opened, however, had what he was looking for: an old-school cassette recorder with a tape of some sort in the deck that had a handwritten label. The fact that it was the kind of cassette you could use to make your own recordings meant that it could be taped over, and that might be the very thing that would save their lives.

"Come over here, you guys," Charlie said. It was a bit of a task for Gordon to move with his cello and still keep the music going. But somehow, he managed. Michelle, however, was beside Charlie almost immediately. It was one of the few times she was thankful her mother had forced her to learn the violin. She had always wanted to play drums in a rock band.

"So what's the big deal?" Gordon asked, a little annoyed that Charlie had dragged him over to look at a cassette player. "I don't think you'll be picking up any news broadcasts on that thing."

"We can record on that," Michelle said, understanding immediately.

"Exactly," Charlie said as he bent over to hit the 'record' button with the hand that wasn't holding his bow. "We might be able to buy ourselves a break with this thing. We just record enough music to fill one side, and then we can concentrate on getting out of here alive without having an instrument in our hands. Turned up to full volume, I'm sure this thing can get louder than we ever thought about."

"Well done, junior. With thinking like that, you might graduate eventually," Gordon said, not as thrilled by the development as he should have been under the circumstances.

"I'm just trying to be as smart as you, maestro," Charlie said, not bothering to hide the snark in his comment. "Now, let's play."

The three of them were uncharacteristically silent as they concentrated on playing as loudly as possible while the wheels of the tape recorder spun lazily. When the recording was finished, Charlie hit the 'rewind' button. The cassette player automatically shut itself off once it reached the beginning of the tape. Hopeful that this might actually work, Charlie hit the 'play' button. The tune they had played was a tired version of Wagner's "Ride of the Valkyries", but the way it roared from the tinny speaker made it sound like it was being performed by the New York Philharmonic.

It was glorious, and the creatures at the windows screeched and fled at the sound.

"It's working," Michelle said, laying her bow and violin down for a moment. "We can stop." She flexed the muscles in her hands and arms. Then, she bent over to touch her toes, stretching her back. "Oh, this feels amazing! You guys have to try this!"

Charlie and Gordon stopped playing too. But they didn't put their instruments down immediately, just in case. Yet, after a few seconds with no attack by the creatures of the deep, both men sat their instruments down and stretched, reveling in such a simple pleasure.

"We need to make a plan quickly," Charlie said as he twisted at the waist and then bent over to stretch the muscles in his lower back. "We don't know how long the batteries will last. We should assume that they aren't fresh."

"What do you suggest?" Michelle asked.

"The first thing I suggest is that Gordon tells us the truth about the piece of music he claims to have written."

Gordon whirled on him. His hands were balled into fists.

"Don't try to deny it," Charlie said. "We should have known better."

"So I didn't write the music," Gordon exclaimed. "Sue me! I was tired of always being overlooked and undervalued. It was my way of getting some attention. How was I supposed to know it would end up this way?"

"What did you do exactly?" Michelle asked.

"It was just an old piece of music that I found. I didn't think anybody would know."

Charlie raced over to a pile of rubble and began throwing chunks of plaster and hunks of floor tile over his shoulder until he found a copy of the music. He ran back to Gordon and Michelle. "And the Latin?"

"Put there by whoever wrote the thing," Gordon said. "I didn't write that."

"Caitlin already translated part of it," Michelle said. "But there is more written at the bottom. I took a couple of years of Latin in college. Let me see if I can tell what it says."

Charlie and Gordon watched her intently. Neither of them could look at each other without glaring. At last,

Michelle spoke. "It's a spell of some sort," she explained. "Playing it let those things loose."

"Is there a way to reverse it?" Charlie asked.

"It doesn't say," Michelle said.

"So we're doomed?" Charlie said. "This is all your fault, Gordon."

Gordon didn't recoil from the accusation. Instead, he nodded solemnly. "I guess it is. But how was I supposed to know what would happen? You can't pin that part on me."

"Maybe not," Charlie said. "But we still wouldn't be in this predicament if you hadn't tried to fake your way into a faculty position."

"Fair point," Gordon said. "So what now?"

Nobody had time to answer. The music coming from the cassette player began to slow down as the batteries were on the verge of failure.

"Everybody get your instruments," Charlie said. "This is our last stand."

Part VI: The End

They made it another hour before Gordon fell from his chair as the physical strain became too much. Charlie and Michelle instinctively backed away from him as the denizens broke in through the busted windows and fell upon Gordon like a pack of hungry dogs. Despite their efforts to play as loudly as possible, they still couldn't escape the wet smacking of lips and the crunch of bone. All that was left of Gordon when the sea creatures were through with him was his cello. The tentacled god beneath the conservatory made short work of that, however, smashing the instrument against the side of the wall with one strong blow. Michelle wept at the sight of the splintered cello and the loss of hope that it represented.

Charlie and Michelle stood beside each other wearily in the corner of the wet, broken practice room. The denizens of the deep had no problem getting in through the windows and door now, but they still couldn't get close enough to stop the music that sputtered from Charlie and Michelle's instruments.

Neither of them wanted to stop playing, but it was apparent that the end was near. Sweat ran down their faces, and their eyes had dark purple crescent moons underneath them. It was hard to imagine that everything had been normal only twelve hours before. That seemed like a lifetime ago.

"They look a little like fish," Charlie noticed, watching the strange beasts with the yellowed eyes stare back at him, opening their mouths every now and then to reveal tiny, sharp teeth like the kind found in the mouth of a piranha.

"They came from the water," Michelle said. "That probably explains part of it."

"No fish I've ever seen can walk on land and murder," Charlie replied. "But that's not really the point, is it?"

"No, it isn't," Michelle said, sorrowful. "The point is that they want to kill us, and there's nothing we can do about it."

"We'll be dead in another hour," Charlie said. "That's my best guess anyway. What do you think?"

Michelle didn't answer.

"Michelle?" Charlie said again.

"I can't go anymore," she whispered before collapsing from the strain of so much continuous playing.

As predicted, the monstrosity beneath the floor reared up from the pit, throwing tentacles in every direction, searching for purchase. Most of the plaster had cracked and fallen away from the ceiling, exposing the joists. The flagella wrapped themselves tightly around the metal railings, and the beast began to pull. At that moment, its only goal was to silence the one instrument that continued to play and to torment.

Charlie was determined that they weren't going to have Michelle. Despite the aching in his wrist, the muscle spasms in his forearms, and the sharp pains that ran all the way up his arm to the shoulder, Charlie stepped in front of Michelle and played for their lives. The denizens, however, kept coming. The music of one wasn't nearly the threat to them that the music of an entire quartet had been.

Charlie said a silent prayer to God and kept playing as barb-laden tentacles and open moray eel mouths rushed toward him and Michelle. The creatures stopped about a foot away. Charlie wrinkled his nose at the smell of ammonia and fish. But there was a stench underlying all of that. It was the rancid odor of dead flesh. It was the smell of Caitlin and Gordon and Professor Grady and so many other friends that hadn't made it. It was the smell of defeat, and Charlie hated it.

The scaly amphibian killers were close enough to touch, but none of them made a move to seize the viola from Charlie's grasp. It was as if an invisible wall or a sheet of glass separated them. The unseen barrier was that of Tchaikovsky and Brahms, and Wagner. It was the litany of long dead gods, and it was all that was saving Charlie and Michelle from destruction. Charlie wasn't about to stop playing.

The denizens opened and closed their mouths like beached fish. It was clear that they were growing impatient. But as long as music still flowed like water, they were limited by their own physiological imperfections. Of course Charlie's tenacity didn't help matters any. It was clear by the way he played that he wasn't going to give up his one chance at happiness.

"Michelle," he said firmly as the joists overhead creaked and groaned.

"I'm exhausted," she replied, struggling to get to her feet.

"Just stay with me a little while longer," he encouraged. "We'll get out of here and start our lives together. We can't give that up."

Although it took a concerted effort, Michelle picked up her bow with trembling hands and began to play again. Immediately, the creatures took a few steps back. They hissed and gurgled to show their irritation.

"Play whatever you can," Charlie told Michelle. "I won't stop no matter what."

Michelle searched Charlie's tired eyes. He wasn't in much better shape than she was, but there was a fierce determination in his gaze that gave her strength. Charlie believed that the two of them could survive, and he was betting their future on it.

Energized by Charlie's attitude and his unyielding hope, Michelle put all of her efforts into her playing. The hideous thing beneath the floor pulled its tentacles back like a frustrated fisherman pulling back his test lines and finding them empty.

"We can do this," Charlie said. "We can."

Michelle smiled, believing in the future for the first time in almost twelve hours. And then something happened to damage that belief.

One of her strings snapped.

Although the nylon-wound string broke with an almost inaudible pop, it could have just as easily been the roar of a cannon in terms of significance.

"Keep playing," Charlie encouraged her. "Don't worry about that string. You've got three others. They'll be enough. They have to be."

Michelle nodded and did as she was told. It was Charlie's turn to break a string ten minutes later.

"If we don't get out of here soon, fatigue won't be our only problem," Michelle said.

Charlie nodded. It was clear that he hadn't wanted to consider that.

"We'll be fine," he said as two of his strings popped in unison.

"I should have put new strings on before we started today," he said as the monsters drew near. "But how could I have known?"

"You couldn't," Michelle said gently.

The two of them looked at each other with a final sense of resolve in their eyes. No amount of struggle would keep them alive. They had fought to survive and lost. Their strength was failing. Their resolve was failing. And now their instruments were failing.

"Well, I guess this is it." Charlie sighed. "Our time is up."

Tears coursed down Michelle's cheeks. She nodded grimly. "I guess so. It's a shame, though. I think we might have been good together."

"I think so too," Charlie agreed.

"So, are we ready to do this?"

"We'll lay down our instruments on three," Charlie said, watching the fish-eyed creatures as they salivated.

"On three," Michelle agreed.

"One," Charlie began.

"Two," Michelle counted.

"Three," Charlie said, laying his instrument down calmly. Michelle did likewise and grabbed his hand. Charlie pulled her close to him and wrapped both arms around her.

For a moment, it was like reality ceased and was encapsulated in glass. Nothing moved. Nothing stirred. Time itself was a fly trapped in amber. Then suddenly, the room was a frenzy of flagellating tentacles and working mouths as the beasts realized that they had their chance.

Once the creatures had eaten their fill and everything was quiet again, the denizens retreated to their underwater lairs where they could sleep and dream in peace, never again to be plagued by the torments of the outside world.

The rush of the ocean whispered silently, punctuated by the occasional squawk of a gull. Gone were the sonatas, the symphonies, the concertos, the operas. Gone were the trills, the runs, and the playing of scales in B flat.

All that was left was the deafening roar of silence.

The Museum Strikes Back

By the time Max had finished reliving the fate of the string quartet through that last vision, he was breathless with excitement and more than a little frightened. His heart thudded inside his chest. A thin trickle of sweat ran from his brow, tracing an erratic path down his cheek.

Max's mind raced, and almost immediately, he made a decision that flew directly in the face of his own personal code as a cat burglar. He decided to quit the job and keep Magnusson's Eye for himself. In all his years as a criminal, he had never done such a thing, and the thought of doing it now made him feel a little dishonest. Which was downright ridiculous when you considered it. Here he was having an internal debate with himself about morals and ethics when the entire nature of his occupation involved breaking and entering and theft.

"Think of this as a means to an end," Max told himself. "Once you make a fortune using this eye, you can quit being a cat burglar and go legit for the rest of your life."

He had always hated himself a little for what he had become, for what he had chosen to do with his life, and the idea of becoming respectable was enough to make his mind up for him. Before he could change his mind and reconsider his position on the matter, Max quickly took a black velvet bag he had brought with him and placed the eye inside. Then, he started toward the exit.

As he crept through the dimly lit hallways of Museum Nocturnus, Max couldn't shake the feeling that he was being watched. But, no, watched wasn't exactly the right word. Stalked was more accurate. He felt like he understood what those gazelles on the Serengeti felt like when a jaguar was nearby. There were a couple of times when he even thought he heard footsteps behind him. Yet, whenever he would stop and look over his shoulder, the museum would always seem empty.

"Beware! Our items are protected!" the signs around the museum read. Yet, in his mind, the words weren't merely spoken, but shouted.

Max considered the nature of the museum, and suddenly a hundred terrifying thoughts came to mind that would explain the feeling of being watched and hunted. This place was filled with haunted and cursed artifacts.

What if the Ouija board in the Hall of Haunted Items had been used to summon something evil from the other side, and that was the presence he felt?

What if all of the dolls in the Hall of Cursed Toys suddenly took up arms and were marching toward him with murderous intent, fueled by whatever spirits possessed them?

What if one of the murder weapons in the Hall of Homicide had some sort of ghostly attachment that was angry about the way it had been robbed of his or her life?

In a museum filled with the macabre, everything looked sinister in the dark. Shadows moved and twisted. Sometimes those shadows took the form of people. Sometimes they took the forms of things that were much, much worse. Max knew it was his imagination. Or at least he hoped it was.

Although the trip from where he had found the eye back to the front door of the museum wasn't that far, the journey took him through several rooms filled with inky blackness. At any moment, he expected something to grab his ankle and pull him down to be feasted upon. It took all he could do not to break into a sprint and run the rest of the way. But he didn't know the layout of this place well, and running would put him at risk of crashing into something, possibly injuring himself and damaging the eye. So, like any good cat burglar, he crept, still hearing the distinctive but faint sound of footsteps behind him every so often.

It was only when he reached the Hall of Murderers that he was gripped by an icy panic that caused him to shiver and tremble involuntarily. At first, he was certain that he was seeing things, that his mind was playing tricks on him. The hall had formerly been filled with the painted portraits of some of Valley Falls' most infamous serial killers. When coming through the first time, Max had noted that the paintings had seemed so lifelike that he had half expected the villains to step out of the frames at any point, brandishing bloodstained knives. Now, the portraits, still framed and hanging in their rightful places on the wall, no longer featured any of the killers. The killers were simply gone as if erased… or escaped.

"Beware! Our items are protected!"

Protected, as he had noted earlier, implied a sort of active defense. Protection hinted at more than just being monitored on camera.

Max realized just what that word meant when he turned to look back the way he had come and saw the doorway filled with the leering faces of all the murderers that had formerly been confined to their prisons of canvas and paint. Gemini, the fiend with the ghastly white face and the leering smile, took the lead, brandishing two knives that gleamed in the faint light given off by the display lights above each painting.

Max screamed as Gemini took one step toward him and then another. The last thing he saw was the rush of homicidal maniacs rushing at him, eager to satiate their bloodlust.

The last thought he had on this earth was this: "Who was B. Thorn, the artist, who had figured out how to bring his paintings to life?"

A few hours later…

Rays of sunshine gradually illuminated Museum Nocturnus, removing some of the menace of the place but not all of it.

Carl, the security guard, who was more of a friendly face than a real protector of the museum's artifacts, unlocked the front door as he did every morning and strolled in with a steaming hot cup of coffee in hand. He was whistling the theme music to The Andy Griffith Show but stopped when he saw the body… or what was left of it.

"Again?" he muttered under his breath and immediately went to the Hall of Murderers. The killers were all back where they belonged in their paintings, brandishing their weapons furiously. Yet, strangely enough, all of them were grinning maniacally this morning, obviously satisfied with themselves. Carl couldn't help noticing that Gemini's knives were bloodstained in the painting today. Normally, they gleamed.

"You guys are killing me," Carl said with a chuckle as he pulled out his phone and prepared to call the authorities. "I don't know why they even bother to keep me on the payroll. I'm obviously not needed."

Soon the place was swarming with cops, CSI, and medical personnel. Also, Magnusson's Eye was back in its rightful place among the other museum's oddities.

And the killers were back in their paintings, sharpening their knives and dreaming malevolent dreams until someone was foolish enough to try and steal something from Museum Nocturnus again.

THE END

About the Author

Jason Brannon is the author of The Cage, Lake October, The Tears of Nero, and several other novels of horror and high strangeness. His short stories have been featured in over 100 publications, translated into German, received the audiobook treatment on occasion, and even won a few awards. He is the co-founder of The Deadbolt Mystery Society but wouldn't dare step foot in Valley Falls. As one of its chief architects, he knows better! He maintains a website at www.jasonbrannon.net.

Made in the USA
Middletown, DE
07 October 2022